Hunting Around
Adventures of a Hunter in The Great Outdoors

Mike Lein

Jackpine Writers' Bloc, Inc.

Other Books By Mike Lein
The "Life at the Cabin" Series

Firewood Happens
Life, Liberty, and the Pursuit of Happiness in Minnesota's Northwoods
A simple book about the simple life. Winner of the Midwest Independent Publishers Association's 2016 Award for Humor.

Down At The Dock
More Stories of the Good Life in the Northwoods
Life at the cabin gets more complicated. A look at serious subjects such as Bigfoot, skinny-dipping, and firewood theft. Winner of the Midwest Independent Publishers Association's 2017 Award for Humor.

The Crooked Lake Chronicles
Mostly True Stories of Life Up North
Lightly embellished tales of the things that happen, the people you meet, and the struggles with Mother Nature that occur when you enjoy the simple life in the Great Outdoors. Finalist for the Midwest Independent Publishers Association's 2019 Award for Humor.

Cabin Fever
Life goes on in the Northwoods
What's an outdoor writer do when he's stuck inside during a pandemic? Write a book about life at the cabin and other adventures in the Great Outdoors. Winner of the Midwest Independent Publishers Association's 2022 Award for Humor.

Jackpine Writers' Bloc, Inc., Publisher
13320 149th Ave
Menahga, MN 56464

Printed in the United States of America
ISBN #978-1-928690-55-9
First Paperback Edition

*Special thanks to The Granddaughter Bailey for the portrait of Sage,
the current Labrador-Retriever-in-Residence.
Cover Photo by Mike Lein.*

Notes and Acknowledgments

It takes more than a writer to make a book happen. Lots of other people contribute from beginning to end. In my case, there's the hard-core members of The Jackpine Writers' Bloc who regularly review my draft writings and offer constructive thoughts on content and other important stuff such as grammar and punctuation. Those last two ain't my specialties.

Also in my case, there's many magazine editors who have seen fit to publish my works on their pages and provide new ideas on structure and voice. Many of the individual stories in this book have benefited from that process. And the checks are welcome too!

Next we have the book editors who bring organization, format, and more editing to the process. In this case I can name names. Sharon Harris and Tarah Wolff of The Jackpine Writers' Bloc Publishing Division have worked with me on five books. I keep going back to them for their expertise.

Finally, some of the stories take advantage of friends and family and their shared experiences with me. Thanks to you for being part of these adventures and for allowing me to share!

Finally, son Andy deserves credit for providing his thoughts on our experiences in "Western Moments" and "Memories." I couldn't have written a better ending myself.

"Many Places to Die" was previously published in edited form in the *Backcountry Journal*, the magazine of the Backcountry Hunters and Anglers.

"Northwoods Mixed Bag," "Blizzard Bird," "After The Shot," "Victory Lap," "Just a Cow," and "Western Moments" were previously published in edited form in *Fur-Fish-Game* magazine.

"Belle Fourche Harry" was previously published in edited form in *The Talking Stick*, the yearly anthology of The Jackpine Writers' Bloc.

"The Montana Mud Dance" and "The Rattler" were previously published in *The Montana Sporting Journal.*

"The Land of the Tape People" was previously published in *Bugle,* the magazine of The Rocky Mountain Elk Foundation.

Foreword

I started my hunting career at an early age, even for a guy of my age. An aunt and uncle provided a well-used pump-action BB gun on my sixth birthday. Add that to the Labrador retriever puppy that was a present the year before and I had everything needed. The farm we lived on became our hunting grounds. Butch and I would roam the buildings and walk the fence lines of the fields, hunting the short list of vermin I was allowed to whang away at with that BB gun. Sparrows and black birds were our main quarry. Pigeons fouling the hay in the loft of the barn were prized "big game."

I managed to down a few despite the nearly worn-out condition of the hand-me-down gun, which spit out BBs so slow you could watch their crooked flight. Nothing went to waste. The farm cats soon learned to follow along. If Butch didn't eat a downed sparrow on the "retrieve," the cats were lined up to fight over the carcass.

This early obsession carried on with many more dogs and guns, and the adventures that come with walking forested trails, watching the natural world go by from a deer stand, or hiking up mountains to see what's there. So far I'm still doing that.

I also grew up reading classic outdoor magazines, jealous of the adventures the writers went on. No doubt these led me to try writing about a few of my own quests with the goal of being published in the same magazines. I have been partially successful in that, perhaps because most of my stories offer editors a change of pace from the usual tales that focus on bagging a trophy, a legal limit of fish, game, or fowl, or thinly veiled advertising for a hot new outdoor product.

I don't mind bagging a big deer or a limit of grouse. But as I age, I've found that a "trophy hunt" doesn't necessarily need a big antlered animal or a pile of game birds to be a true quality hunt. Some of those adventures are included in my first four books—the "Life at the Cabin" series. Here's a few more, all put together in one place. So enjoy these and then get out there and have a few of your own adventures.

Table of Contents

Hunting Around

Prologue

Many Places to Die—
A Conversation with
Bob the Reaper

The fumes of penetrating oil stain hung heavy in the air as I knelt to brush the bottom rows of the cabin's log siding. I was light-headed from inhaling the nasty stuff for most of the afternoon. But it was a dirty job that needed to be done before I got busy with hunting season. That's when an unfamiliar voice weighed in from behind me.

"Hey, Mike—got a minute to talk?"

I dropped the brush in surprise, swore, picked the messy thing up from the dirt and leaves, and turned to see who needed to be dealt with. Here was a serious-looking guy in a blue suit, white shirt, and red power tie. Given that it was September in an election year, I assumed the worst. Not just some traveling salesman or door-to-door religious type. Another damn politician.

I tried to be Minnesota Nice. "So what's there to talk about? I already know who I'm voting for."

The stranger looked surprised, glanced down at his suit, and then started right in. "No. No. I'm not a politician. Shoulda thought about that. Let me change."

He didn't say "Abracadabra," snap his fingers, or even make some sort of "poof" sound. His clothes and appearance just changed in an instant and now he was wearing a plaid shirt and jeans and had longer hair and a three-day beard.

I started backing away, eyes wide, dripping stain

1

brush in hand, stuttering—"Whaaaaatttt the Helll . . ."

"Hey, hey—sorry about that! I'm friendly!" The guy fast-talked. "It's not your day today—I just need to get some info. Won't take long; just stay calm, don't freak out!"

Throwing the brush at him and running for the woods seemed like a good idea. Yet somehow I held my ground.

"Who the hell are you? How did you do that? And what do you mean, 'it's not my day'?"

The guy laid down his sales pitch. "Don't worry about the change thing—that's not important. I had to get your attention; just bear with me. You can call me Bob. Let me explain a few things."

"Ok, 'Bob.' Try me."

He kept up the fast talk. "Look, there's no easy explanation. Call me your Guardian Angel if that helps but, I'm more like your personal Grim Reaper. I help people die. It's not your day today; just stay calm, and hear me out."

Now if it hadn't been for that appearance-change thing, he was just another crazy guy in the woods. I felt a sudden urge to take a leak and tried to think of escape routes while talking for distraction. "So you're 'Bob the Reaper'? Where's your black cloak and scythe?"

"We gave them up a while back. Part of our Death Improvement Plan. That outfit scared some people to death when all we wanted to do was talk. 'Bob' isn't my real name. You couldn't pronounce that. Now here's the deal. Us reapers made a proposal to the guys in charge. We asked to do a survey about making the death experience and our jobs less scary."

"The guys in charge? Don't you mean 'The Guy'?"

"I just report on up the chain like everyone else. We have some new ideas."

"Ok—like what?"

He moved a little closer and went on with the sales pitch. "A bunch of us want to gather info. Like asking people where they would like to die when the time comes. Sometimes we can arrange that. Think about it. You wouldn't know when your number's up. But it could be quick and easy in your favorite place. It might cut back on the pain and anguish. And your friends could say —'Well, at least he died happy.' "

"Let me get this straight. I could pick where and when I die?"

"No, can't control the 'When.' That's way above my pay grade and authority."

"Your authority? You say you're The Reaper!"

"Just one of many," he said. "And I follow orders from above like everyone else."

Now this was starting to get interesting even if he was nuts. "Who's above you?" I asked.

"That," said Bob, "is information provided only on a need-to-know basis. And you don't need to know until your number is up. Want me to speed that up to satisfy your curiosity?"

"No! No! I can wait!"

"Thought so . . ." Bob got down to business.

Hunting Around

"Times a-wasting and there's no overtime at this job. Name me a few places where you wouldn't mind dying. And your cabin here don't count. For Christ's sake, you've written about this place enough. People get it. Move on!"

"Hey—I like it here!" I looked out over the lake, shining in the mid-day sun, thinking while still trying to get my head straight about this interruption in an otherwise ordinary day.

"Ok, here's an easy one. How about out in the forest on a spring morning, turkey hunting, having a cup of coffee while the sun rises, with the turkeys gobbling and all the birds singing after being gone for the winter?"

"Now that's what I'm talking about—great details!" Bob exclaimed. "That's close to the cabin but good. Now think. It can't be in the past. Even we haven't figured out time travel yet. No going back to college and dying in the arms of some old girlfriend. And what the hell were you thinking when you took up with that lawyer back then?"

Now that was low and scary at the same time. *How much did this guy know?* "I had no idea she wanted to be a lawyer. And in my defense, I dumped her!"

"Sure." Bob nodded. "Keep thinking that. Now come on, you've traveled the world. There must be somewhere farther away. We need data, points to compare and sort out."

A few scenes from past adventures ran through my mind. That beach in France in the fog? Nice, but it had crabby French people. Iceland maybe. On the beach by Olafsvik or even the Snaefellsjokull Glacier?

Bob tipped his hand here. I'd say he can definitely read minds. "Don't go for Iceland. Too damn many trolls and fairies messing with the process—can't stand them. How about you focus and stay with the hunting theme? Got to move things along here!"

An upcoming trip to Montana popped into my mind. "Is Montana far enough away? There's that old, deserted cabin out on the prairie. It's got mountains in the background and deer and antelope running around. My bones would fit right in with that scene."

"Ok—that's two. Progress. Keep it up. How about another Montana one just to speed things up here."

"I'm thinking—this is hard. How about that ridge out there overlooking the Missouri River? Elk bugling at sunrise, a cup of coffee, and my favorite rifle."

"So," Bob asked, "which is your favorite rifle? Your collection is getting out of hand. How many guns does one guy need?"

"What are you, my wife?" I challenged him. Then backed down when a bit of evil glinted in his eyes. Might have gone too far with that one . . .

He wagged a finger at me. "Stay calm—just pointing out the obvious. It's that old Husqvarna bolt-action anyway. You've written about that enough too. Now hurry up—the clock's ticking."

"I might have chosen one of the muzzleloaders, but I could live with the Husqvarna. Or actually die with it, I guess."

"Cut the comedy. You don't think this is serious business? What's next?"

5

Hunting Around

"Maybe walking back in the forest in October, hunting grouse with a nice side-by-side shotgun and the dog. Or maybe deer hunting there after some fresh snow. Just looking for stuff and exploring."

Bob shook his head. "What the hell . . . What's with the snow thing? I like it hot myself. Hotter than you can imagine."

This time I gave him the look. "So there really is a 'hot place'?"

"It's not what you think," he said. "I don't sit around with the Devil in his lava hot tub. I just like it hot."

"Sooooo—there is a Devil?"

He gave me a pained look. "Need-to-know basis. And I can speed that up. One more and make it fast."

That brought up a few more questions but I tried to stay focused, keep things simple and on this continent. "How about over at the Farm? Sitting at the kitchen table with the guys, sipping brandy and eating fresh venison liver? It's like a cabin but not this one. That's five. Want more?"

"No," he said. "You talk too much, just like you write too much. Let's end it now before you get real wound up. You might hear from me again, might not. Depends on the people upstairs. They got a lot on their minds. They can't even hire enough reapers for the work."

"You need more reapers?"

"Yeah—think about it. More people every day. More people getting in trouble every day. More people dying every day. And you aren't necessarily alone in the universe."

That got my interest. But he waved my unspoken questions off.

"Need-to-know basis! Now since you didn't keel over dead when I showed up, here's some tips that might earn you some points and a few more years. Go to church more often. Pastor Eric notices and you get extra points for that stuff. Eat better, drink less, exercise, and stay off the cell phone when you're driving. Living longer ain't exactly rocket science. Any questions?"

"Well—quite a few. So there really is a Heaven?"

He gave me that pained look one last time —"Need-to-know . . . And by the way—mistaking me for a politician didn't get you any extra points. Be careful who you call that."

Then he was gone. No poof. No fade out. No Starship Enterprise transporter sound and sparkling lights. Just gone, leaving me standing in front of the cabin with a dripping brush in hand, the stink of oil stain thick in the air, feeling a little weak and chilled.

Real experience? Dream? Hallucination from the oil fumes? I'm not sure. But real or not, I'm in no hurry to see Bob the Reaper again anytime soon. I've got a few more places to check out first.

UP NORTH

Sage

Bailey Haseley

Northwoods Mixed Bag

Northwoods Mixed Bag

Oldest son, Andy, and I parked the truck at the lake access, let the eager dogs out, and readied our guns while discussing strategy. On this mid-October morning, surrounded by thousands of acres of Minnesota state forest, we had a mix of potential targets in mind. This particular spot was a water-surrounded peninsula with a small lake on the east, a swampy channel along the south boundary, and a large weedy pond on the west.

We'd done this before, so I offered up the usual plan. "I'll take the dogs up the road and come in through the middle of the woods. You head up the shore to the beaver house and hang out. There should be wood ducks in the channel. If the dogs and I jump a grouse on the way in and take a shot, the ducks should spook out right past you."

Andy headed up the shore while I walked Tikka, Andy's young yellow Lab, and Kal, my trusty twelve-year-old black Lab, back down the logging road. I waited a few minutes for Andy to get into position and then turned the dogs loose for the sneak through the forest. Kal quartered in front, nose to the ground, with Tikka shadowing her. We only made it about thirty yards when the action started.

A ruffed grouse started running across the fallen aspen leaves with Kal hot behind, chasing it like a chicken across a farm yard. She forced it to flush up into the thick

13

bamboo-like aspen regrowth from logging five years ago. The grouse fought to clear the cover, wings rattling off branches. The load of steel 8s from my double-barrel caught up before it cleared the tops.

I dropped another shell into the gun and urged Kal toward the downed bird. That put a woodcock into the air just in front of me, twittering up over the aspens and leveling off towards the oak ridge ahead. This time I used both barrels and the bird kept on going.

Kal and Tikka headed back with the grouse and flushed another woodcock on the way. This bird went right and tumbled down with my first shot. Kal handed over the grouse and headed for the woodcock, flushing another grouse in the process. That one caught me flat-footed, dead bird in hand and the gun broke open in the middle of reloading. It thundered off without a shot.

About that time Andy's shotgun started booming back at the lake. Three rapid shots, soon followed by three more. The dogs and I pushed ahead through the aspens and the dogwood and hazelnut brush to join the action. I reloaded at the edge of the woods, quickly transferring 3-inch steel 4s into the chambers before stepping out to the grassy edge of the open channel. I was hoping for a late-flushing wood duck. That didn't happen but Kal put a jack-snipe into the air, squawking, twisting, and dipping away. I waited for it to get out a ways and dropped it into the lily pads with the improved cylinder barrel. Kal chugged out through the weeds, grabbed the small bird, and brought it back to hand without apparent thoughts of "what the heck is this?" We then continued up the channel and around the point to where Andy was watching two wood ducks floating belly up. This time Tikka got some action too.

This short hunt showed the beauty of hunting in Minnesota's Northwoods in October. Plenty of public land to hunt and plenty of variety when it comes to game birds. It's entirely possible to shoot ruffed grouse, woodcock, several types of ducks, and even big Canada geese within yards of each other. And then there's the squirrels, snowshoe hares, turkeys, and even jack-snipe if you care for real variety. It's also a place where both the versatility of the Labrador retriever as a gun dog and the practicality of a double-barrel shotgun are on display.

About twenty-five years ago, my wife and I purchased five acres on a small lake in northern Minnesota. I wanted a place that provided fishing and swimming for family fun in the summer. I also wanted a location where I could grab a gun, call a dog, and be hunting almost immediately. Our land sits on the edge of thousands of acres of state forest and fits that bill. Construction of a small semi-rustic cabin started soon after the purchase. It's the place to be come fall and hunting season, especially in October during the small game and waterfowl season.

The surrounding forest is a mixture of aspen, birch, oak, and maple with a fair amount of red and white pine mixed in. This is the heart of Minnesota's lake country. Sprinkled throughout the forest are small lakes without formal names, beaver ponds, and alder-ringed grassy swamps. The edges of these hold grouse year-round and woodcock during the fall migration. The open water attracts local Canada geese, wood ducks, ring-neck ducks, and some mallards.

Hunting these small waters is one of the most productive ways to get ducks after opening day. Pressure on popular lakes and swamps sends local ducks looking for places to hide. Andy and I started that morning on a small lake, using waders to set a dozen decoys off a point. The sun rose to create a typical beautiful fall day with sunshine, colorful autumn foliage, and the promise of fifty-degree temperatures later on. Nice weather. But not the kind that generates a memorable hunt with flock after flock of waterfowl setting wings into a decoy spread.

We got a few early shots at skittish wood ducks and I dropped a lone goldeneye that screamed past overhead. That's it. Within a half-hour after sunrise the scarce action got scarcer. The waterfowl migration was not yet in full swing and the local ducks had all those small ponds to hide out on until colder weather iced them up. We picked up the decoys and went looking for action.

These hunts are much more productive if you have a good dog or dogs accompanying you. Hunting ducks and grouse is possible without a dog if you are willing to get cold and wet skinny-dipping for a downed duck. You will also be passing on the healthy woodcock population that lives and migrates through the area. Woodcock are near impossible to flush without a dog.

I won't claim that a Labrador retriever is the only dog that will work in these hunts. That is a subject for late night campfire and hunting camp table discussions where some guys will point out that Labs can tend to roam a bit far ahead for grouse and most don't point. However, they willingly adapt to this type of hunting. They might not point or retrieve a woodcock, but they will flush them, find downed birds, and patiently wait for you to walk over and stuff them in the vest. They will also be a willing participant in a cold icy duck blind later in the season when the small ponds have frozen and decoys over big water are the only option for late-season ducks and geese.

I've also found that a double-barrel shotgun shines on these hunts. I haven't talked either of my sons into converting to double-barrels just yet. They both carry 12-gauge pumps with choke tubes and 3½-inch chambers. These are versatile, dependable, and might have an edge over a double gun in a traditional duck blind over decoys. But I dearly love side-by-side shotguns for this mixed bag, mixed cover hunting and not just because I'm some sort of romantic throwback.

The gun I was carrying that day was a 12-gauge side-by-side double-barrel equipped with a set of aftermarket choke tubes. It's been used to bag everything from the jack-snipe in this story to a half-dozen turkeys and a bunch of geese. It's a short handy gun that I'm not afraid to knock around in a duck blind or push through brush.

A typical hunt unfolds like this. In our area, mid-October brings in a decent migration of woodcock to mix in with the local grouse. And as mentioned before, the local ducks have found out-of-the-way places to loaf and feed. So we pick out a spot that has a mixed cover of aspen re-growth, grassy alder-ringed swamps, and an open pond or small lake that's off-road and hidden. We walk the aspen regrowth and the edges of the swamps on the way to the pond, letting the dogs do their work. If a woodcock or grouse flushes, we don't hesitate to take a shot. This will likely spook any ducks off the open water ahead but as the saying goes: a woodcock in the hand is better than maybe a shot at a wood duck on a pond.

There's one other tactic that's worth trying. One of the most common ducks in our area, next to the wood duck, is the ring-neck or "ring-bill." Small family flocks are common on lakes and ponds in October, taking advantage of the wild rice and pond celery. They can be very curious and susceptible to that age-old practice of "tolling." If we spot an undisturbed flock out of range, we hunker down in the weeds and start throwing sticks out into the open water.

The Labs will do what Labs will do. They happily retrieve the sticks just like the thousands of dummies and tennis balls retrieved from the dock all summer. The splashing and commotion often gets the ducks interested enough to swim over into easy range.

Recently Andy and I set off on another of these mixed bag adventures. In this case I was carrying a percussion muzzleloading 12-gauge shotgun stuffed with non-toxic #6 shot, just to add to the fun. We worked uphill through a series of grassy muddy beaver ponds, with the dogs hunting the alder fringe for grouse and woodcock. Up ahead was the final pond of the series. A small tight area with a strip of open water full of beaver logs and weeds, prime stuff for wood ducks. No grouse or woodcock showed up this time to spook the ducks.

We paused below the final beaver dam. I held onto the dogs while Andy reloaded with duck loads and then peeked up over the rim of the dam. He ducked back quickly and turned to me with wide eyes. "Mallards!" he whispered. "A bunch of them! Right in front of us!"

I moved up alongside him, turned loose the dogs and we stepped forward over the dam together. What greeted us could have been the cover picture for a waterfowl hunting calendar. A yellow Lab and a black Lab charging into the water, perhaps thirty big mallards quacking alarms as they jumped into the air just yards away, climbing straight up in the clear blue sky with water splashing and falling from bright plumage, green heads and orange feet all shining in the October sun.

I picked a greenhead climbing to the left and unloaded the right barrel in his general direction. He came out from behind the smoke cloud unscathed. I stuck with him and let the left hammer drop, struggling to gauge his steep rate of climb and to stay focused while other ducks scattered around behind him. He lived to fly away and swim in another swamp.

Andy was frantically working that pump gun alongside me, struggling as I did with a little "duck fever" and the chaos of many targets in a small area. When it was all over, the dogs had nothing to fetch.

In Andy's defense, he and Tikka returned to the same pond the next day and found that a smaller flock had returned. He doubled on a nice pair of greenheads and regained some of his self-confidence. But for now, all we could do was stand on the dam shaking our heads, watching all those big beautiful mallards fly away. Once we calmed down, he looked at me and asked the obvious. "What the hell happened there?"

I suppose I could have claimed an excuse. After all, I was shooting a muzzleloader. But I had to be honest. "I don't know. But we are going to remember that for a long time!"

The Cowboy Gun

The Cowboy Gun

Believe it or not, at one point in my life I was rather gun-poor. This situation has long since been remedied, probably to excess according to wife Marcie. But this story begins with me perched in an oak tree, many years ago, with "The Cowboy Gun" in my cold, freezing, nearly lifeless hands. And I mean perched. This was also before the days of mass-produced tree stands, safety harnesses, and a smarter, safer me.

The sun peeked over the horizon and tried to melt through the forest. As most northern climate hunters have learned, sunrise is when the temperature seems to drop to rock bottom and chill to the bone. I was shivering. My feet were numb. My fingers were losing feeling. I was reconsidering the folly of sitting on an oak limb fifteen feet above the ground in November. Then came the sound of big animals crunching through the frozen forest.

Two deer hurried across a small frosty grass-covered swamp a hundred yards to the south, one following the other. The trailing one flashed antlers in the bright, suddenly much warmer sun before disappearing into cover. I swung around on my awkward perch and hoped they kept coming. Several anxious minutes later, the lead deer materialized out of the swamp fringe and slowly moved through the oak grove twenty yards away.

I was tempted. It was obviously a big adult doe,

the buck was not visible, and I was very venison-poor at the time. But I waited and hoped the buck would follow. Once in a great while these things work out the way we hope and dream that they will. He cautiously peeked out of the thick stuff, antlers shining and growing larger every minute. Somehow I was able to hold back until he eased into the clear and turned broadside to follow the doe. The hammer was back and ready. I pulled the trigger and let it drop. The eight-pointer dropped too, literally right in his tracks when the 170-grain soft nose broke his spine just behind the shoulder. I am lucky I didn't break my own back scrambling down out of that tree.

I don't know much about the history of the gun I was carrying that day. My modern bolt action and scope-toting hunting partners had dubbed it "The Cowboy Gun" when I showed up at the Farm. It looked like something John Wayne should be carrying in an old western movie. A used-but-not-abused Marlin 1893 .30-30 with "Special Smokeless" stamped into the blue metal of the octagon-barrel.

It came to the forests of Minnesota from the mountains of western Oregon via my step-grandfather Ted. He handed it off to my favorite uncle. Uncle Fred was the one who found and financed my first shotgun, my first .22, and my first deer rifle. He passed this gun on to me one Christmas when two things became obvious. His hunting days were over but he had helped me develop a lifelong passion.

This old veteran is a semi-rare takedown model, capable of being split in half at the receiver to lessen the liability of its forty-inch length. It has other liabilities. Shove nine 170-grain loads up the tubular magazine running the full length of that long barrel and it is decidedly nose heavy. Which is not a totally bad thing given the old-fashioned buckhorn sights which tend to make you shoot high when things happen real quick.

I bet the gun could tell a few stories about the good old days in the Old West. Internet gun gurus tell me its serial number and markings indicate a production date of somewhere around 1908. They also tell me that its overall good condition and the special take-down feature means a monetary value of around twenty times more than it cost new.

It could have been Grandpa Ted's first rifle, purchased brand new in a small town hardware store with hard-earned cash or handed to him as a present by a proud father or maybe even a rite-of-passage gift from a favorite uncle. I have always imagined him stalking elk in the wet and misty rain forest of Oregon or mule deer in the arid eastern foothills or trekking back to Minnesota to hunt whitetails in the Northwoods. While I never got a chance to ask him about his stories, I do know it has created new ones in my hands. It even starred in another story on the same day as the eight-pointer mentioned at the beginning.

Minnesota allows party hunting—legally bagging and tagging deer for agreeable members of your hunting group. That year my buddies and I only had two days to hunt, extra tags to fill, and plenty of mouths to feed back home. We were all in favor of filling those tags any way we could. So I didn't head back to camp and start washing dishes after bagging that big buck. I kept hunting.

Mid-afternoon found me exploring a long narrow finger of woods, walking the ice of the swamp that lined the interior. I reached the end of the woods and paused to plan the next move. That's when a huge deer wearing a respectable set of antlers reared up out of a tangle of deadfalls only spitting distance away and attempted to get the hell out of there real fast.

I thumbed the hammer back as the gun came up. But not far enough. It slipped off my thumb, dropped, and the gun boomed a big round-nosed bullet off into the atmosphere towards the moon. I'm quite sure there were curses as I worked the long throw lever, racked another shell in, and lowered the gun again. The gun boomed at close range just as the buck broke free of the tangled mess he had hidden in. I worked the lever, fired a third time, and saw him flinch. I was cranking in a fourth round when he reached the edge of the woods and went down face-first into the plowed field. At first I thought he was merely going low, scooting under a high wire fence. But he never got up. Both aimed shots had punched through his chest and this gray-faced old ten-pointer was now the biggest deer I had ever shot, next to the eight-pointer taken earlier.

Thus ended what was likely the best day of deer hunting I will ever have. That gun and I were legends in our deer camp for a few short years. However, stories of The Cowboy Gun and me don't end there and they don't all involve a hero shot of me with a dang big buck.

The Cowboy Gun

I have noticed that for some reason this gun shoots much better when I am alone and without witnesses and it shoots horribly when I am in the company of others. Others who seem to easily forget or gloss over those big bucks bagged by myself. They remember only what they have witnessed in person. My so-called hunting buddies, the same guys that helped me drag two big bucks on one day, keep reminding me of another morning in those same woods.

After a slow opening morning, four of us met for an early lunch at "The Funnel," a point at the west edge of the Farm where woods are pinched together on the west by "The Lake," on the east by "The Bog," and open to a field on the north. We sat in the shadows, just inside the woods, planning the afternoon hunt while we chewed on sandwiches and drank coffee. I looked across the alfalfa field to the north and dreamed of a huge buck with antlers branching upward like an expensive candelabra, polished tips glowing in the sunshine like lit candles.

It suddenly dawned on stupid me that I wasn't dreaming. There was just such a buck, less than half a football field away and walking rapidly across the field to us.

"Don't move!" I hushed the others. They looked up, saw the buck, and froze. My dream was their nightmare, their guns all carelessly out of reach while I had The Cowboy Gun still in my hands. The buck heard my hushed voice and stopped, broadside, twenty-five yards out. He looked unconcerned as I lowered the old lever gun in his direction, unaware that he was about to become a legend.

"Remember, shoot low!" my buddy Steve hissed, literally looking over my shoulder as I pulled the trigger. The gun boomed. The buck whirled, suddenly concerned, and bounded back across the field with tail held high and flagging. I worked the lever again, again, again, and again, chasing him across the field with what I thought were well-aimed bullets. But remember that little problem mentioned earlier about shooting high in stressful situations? The same problem Steve had just thoughtfully reminded me of? It apparently reared its ugly head here since an exhaustive search soon indicated that those bullets had not touched a hair on that big boy's body.

Some things have changed at our hunting camp in the years since. My buddies and I prefer to fill our own tags these days and are less desperate for venison and time. Hunting deer and hanging out together at the Farm seem to be more important now than simply killing deer. And I have many more firearm options at my disposal.

But there's always hope I will run across that buck's relatives and finally silence my friends. Because while that buck might have escaped The Cowboy Gun and me that day, the story lives on. My hunting buddies bring up that incident every November when we come together. Just because that big buck escaped, doesn't mean he was forgotten.

Blizzard Bird

The thermometer on the cabin's deck is reading twenty-four degrees at 3:45 AM. An almost full moon shines down, casting moon shadows of bare trees across the yard. All this is about to change. The weatherman on last night's news called for a winter storm warning with up to a foot of snow. Given that forecast, I pull on warm duck-hunting outerwear and winter ice fishing boots before starting the truck. I am not hunting ducks or ice fishing today. It's April and the opening day of turkey season, just a little bit south of Canada.

It might surprise some people to learn that Minnesota has pretty good turkey hunting—and not just in the balmy southern portion of the state. Eastern-strain turkeys were introduced to southeastern Minnesota in the early 1970s. They took off from there, expanded to the north and west, and in some areas can now be hunted all the way to Canada. My rustic cabin is tucked away on the edge of thousands of acres of state forest a couple of hours south of the border. Turkeys have become regulars in the driveway, at the bird feeders, and on forest roads despite winter temperatures that drop below zero regularly and hit minus thirty pretty often.

These birds are tough and adaptable and hunt just like any other turkey across the state. The weather, on the other hand, can throw you some curves. Some years I've hunted in a camo T-shirt, battling ticks and mosquitoes while looking for shade. And I've hunted on days with even worse weather forecasts than today's.

Luckily, I know about a little place. A place where I have taken several other hunters to bag their first turkeys. A place where pine and hardwood forest meets with scattered farm fields. A place that always seems to hold birds, even in bad weather. It's a honey hole I have confidence in.

I pull off the road onto a logging trail well before shooting time and with plenty of time to set up while listening for gobbles in the moonlight. I strap on my turkey vest preloaded with calls, decoys, and ammo, grab the blind and a folding chair with one hand and the gun with the other. Loggers have been hard at work thinning the orderly rows of the pine plantation. The logging slash covering the ground turns the trail into a moonlit obstacle course.

Northern turkeys aren't afraid to travel, so being mobile is usually a good idea. I like to travel light, moving around, using deadfalls and other cover for natural blinds. However, with today's forecast, a cozy camo blind is a reasonable backup plan. A spot one hundred yards from the edge of a private farm field and another fifty yards from a brushy swamp looks good. Even if the weather keeps the birds from feeling frisky, they might funnel through this area.

With the blind staked out and a jake and a hen decoy in place, it's time to get quiet and listen. Most often there's a flock a quarter of a mile to the northwest, safely roosting in a stand of tall red pines on private land. Others may roost near the lake a half-mile to the west. The woods here seem to be the sweet spot where the hens come together in mid-morning to scratch in the pine needles while the toms strut their stuff.

About this time the weatherman proves he can be right part of the time. First the wind ramps up, roaring through the tops of the pines. Then the clouds roll in to cover the moon and the first light of dawn and the real fun starts. Neither snow nor rain. Sleet. I give up my romantic idea of an active run-and-gun hunt, make sure the blind is securely staked, and tuck in to hide from the weather.

One of the many reasons I like this spot is the other activity that happens while waiting for turkeys. A spring wildlife show usually plays out on the field, in the pines, and overhead in the sky. Whippoorwills shout out their name. Porcupines waddle past. Red squirrels challenge from the pines, their beady little eyes not fooled by camo clothing. Sandhill cranes flap over, eagles and ospreys screech, geese honk, deer play hide-and-seek, and every kind of small migrating songbird flutters by. Today none of that is happening as daylight slowly arrives. A raven croaking is the only sound audible above the gusting wind.

It's times like this when memories of previous hunts keep hope alive. Like a beautiful spring afternoon with my oldest son. I called in a flock of jakes minutes before we had to head for home. Andy overcame a bad case of turkey fever, shot his first turkey, and has tagged a bird just about every season since.

Hunting Around

Another time a huge old tom taught me a lesson about turkeys and assumptions. I called him in from across the field, working him into a frenzy with a cheap plastic box call. He busted through low hanging pine branches, his head lit up like a red, white, and blue softball, absolutely crazy to find the hen I was pretending to be. I held my fire and let him come within ten yards, wondering how he would react to my decoy. He spotted it, ended his strut in mid-step and ran back the way he came. A 2-ounce load of 4s chased him through the brush without harming a feather. He left behind a frustrated turkey hunter vowing to never again pass up an easy shot.

Other hunts had their own weather-related challenges. I took my brother-in-law and youngest son here together on their first turkey hunt. We hunted the aftermath of a big blizzard, using a sled to haul a blind and heater into the trees. Decoys were propped up on top of waist-deep snow banks. The only excitement was provided by other wildlife trying to survive in the same conditions. A goshawk slammed into a hen decoy from above and then hung around, staring at it, trying to figure out what had just happened. More exciting was the wolf that snuck in to my brother-in-law's turkey calls. Dale and the wolf departed at equal speed in opposite directions.

With these memories, and plenty of coffee and snacks, the first three hours pass by. I work the calls, usually beating hard on a big loud box call in hopes it can be heard over the wind. The sleet turns to snow that melts as it hits the ground but gradually turns the decoys white. I have to almost fully close the blind's windows to keep the wet snow from sliding down the roof and into my lap.

The first hint of hope comes right at ten o'clock —a halfhearted, barely audible gobble carried in on the northeast wind. I fumble for the call and try to power a sexy cackle through the wind. No response comes back through the snowflakes driven horizontally past the blind. About this time the weather finds my Achilles's heel, chilling my feet despite insulated winter boots.

My faith in this honey hole remains strong. I tough it out. Several years ago I was here, hunting from a natural blind in a half-foot of snow and twenty degree temperatures. By noon I was chilled to the bone. Then two huge old toms walked across the field two hundred yards away, beards dragging in the snow and making me forget the cold.

I tried a cackle on my box call. They stopped, looked my way, and then continued off to the edge of the forest. I popped in a mouth call and tried my best "pee-pee-pee, chuck-chuck-chuck," hoping a pleading young hen might bring them sneaking back. That didn't happen. But minutes later, two jakes walked across the field, following in the footsteps of the toms. I tried the mouth call on them.

They stopped, saw the decoys, and came running like road runners being chased by Wile E. Coyote. One of them slammed on his brakes right in front of a decoy and went into a strut. I took the shot and took him back to the cabin to cool off on the deck while I warmed up in front of the woodstove.

By 11:30 my feet can't take the cold any longer. I

ease out of the blind and slowly sneak north towards the weak gobble heard earlier. The wind is still blowing flakes sideways, limiting visability to a couple hundred yards even in the shelter of the pines. I tuck along the edge of an alder swamp, using the thick brush for a wind break until reaching a corner where there's a view across the plantation. Huddling against a pine, I pull out that big loud box call and pound a cackle off through the pines.

Nothing answers back. But a large black bird comes flying through the snow flakes towards me. "Raven," I think. "Maybe eagle." It disappears into the thick branches of a lone white pine on the far edge. I do another cackle. The big black bird drops out the pine, goes into full turkey strut, and booms a crazy gobble back at me.

That gobble makes me forget all about the weather and cold numb hands and feet. I slide down the tree, dropping out of sight below piles of logging slash, and hit the call once more.

He's less than one hundred yards away and things are happening fast as he gobbles back and starts trotting down a row of pines. At fifty yards he struts and stretches to listen. I give a few soft clucks on the call and he starts trotting again, heading for an opening twenty yards away. I ease the double-barrel up and shoulder it just as he steps into the clear.

A big glob of wet fluffy snow is hanging off the right barrel of the gun but the sight picture looks good, right above the base of the neck, below his glowing head. I pull the trigger and get smacked hard by the recoil of a magnum 3 ½ inch load of 4s.

The tom jumps straight up in the air and comes down, staggering but not down, ducking below the slash piles and disappearing. He clears the slash thirty yards out, still moving until my second shot sends him head first, wings flapping into the snow. I hustle over to him and sit down in the pines to admire him and relive the hectic last minutes, stashing those memories away.

I do my best to get decent pictures of the tom and the setting. After all, while I probably will be hunting turkeys in bad weather again, another one probably won't fly to me through a blizzard. He's a nice hefty bird with a 9 1/2-inch beard and 1-inch plus spurs. He looks good in the pictures. Me, I'm not so sure. I should have taken off my winter face mask for the photo shoot. But when you're hunting turkeys in a blizzard in the Great White North, it's better to be warm than good looking.

Recommitment

Recommitment

I flopped down on the couch with a good beer, still strung out from the three-hour drive home from the cabin. Marcie has already heard the short version of the weekend adventures via cell phone. "Why," she asks, "can you shoot all kinds of deer at the Farm, but you can't get one at the cabin?"

The answer doesn't take much thought. "It's ALL different," I say. "At the Farm we're hunting from stands, with modern rifles, in a confined area, with other hunters. The deer come to us. At the cabin, I'm hunting thousands of acres of big woods, by myself, with a muzzleloader. It's one-on-one with the deer, on their own terms, with two-hundred-year-old technology."

Deer hunting at the Farm was, and still is, not overly challenging, especially if you are there for the atmosphere and "a deer," not necessarily "The Deer." I bought my 54-caliber muzzleloader over thirty years ago and committed myself to the challenge of using it at least one day of the rifle season. Over the next ten years or so I used it to bag multiple deer. One was a swollen-necked eight-point buck that could not resist trailing a doe to within fifteen yards of my tree stand. The gun also generated its share of stories including the infamous tale of the broken ram rod.

But my commitment suffered over time. In recent years I used it only sporadically. I had excuses. More people hunting the Farm, other guns to play with, less time for tune up on the range. I carried it on a couple of late season forays into the woods near the cabin without ever expecting to fire it. It was more of an excuse to be in the woods alone in December. Excuses, excuses. When I start arguing with myself and making excuses, I know it's time to look deep within.

So this year I recommitted myself to the original reasons for the gun—one shot, close up, hunting by myself, with a firearm that involves skills more complicated than simply dropping a brass cartridge into a chamber. My sons had already put three deer in the freezer by the time the muzzleloader season arrived. I headed north to the cabin, hunting for a "luxury" deer that could be used for pepper sticks, sausage, jerky, and other good stuff. I was also hunting for revenge for all the newly planted white pines the vermin had eaten and, most important, for the experience itself.

Saturday. The first morning is just about as miserable as early December in the Minnesota Northwoods can get. The only element lacking is some sort of precipitation. Overcast, thirty-mile-per-hour howling north wind, and zero degrees. I am tempted to stay in the cabin with my fresh pot of coffee. But I stoke the wood burner to keep Marcie and the dog warm and carry a folding chair and a big jug of coffee to a hillside near the cabin. I sense a slow start to the season as the woods come to life. The usual chickadees and blue jays show but the wind keeps the deer in their beds. The walk back to the cabin shows the tracks of one very small

Bambi on the driveway in the two-day-old snow.

Marcie drops me off at a logging road a mile from the cabin after a quick trip to town. This is public land but there is absolutely no sign of other hunters and ample deer sign in the snow. I follow the primitive road to the south end of the lake and start sneaking along the western shore.

"Sneaking" is probably a bad choice of words. The snow crunches on the ice with every step. Deer are bedded down on a sunny hillside out of the wind. But they hear and see me first. A buck leaps from its bed and crosses a small opening with respectable antlers shining in the sun. Several more follow. The hammer is back, the gun is up, but none of them provides a decent shot. A couple more steps forward—one final deer leaves a bed, pauses, but not long enough, and is gone into the thick brush. The final half-mile to the cabin produces a flushing grouse, mink tracks, and an otter huffing and splashing water from a hole in the lake bank.

The late evening hunt is anticlimactic. I walk my driveway to access the forest north of the cabin. The ten-year-old logged-over forest is dense with spindly aspen that limits visibility even with the snow. No new tracks are showing. Just filled-in outlines of several-days-old ones. I wait out the afternoon on a beaver-felled tree overlooking a pond and walk out in the final light.

Sunday—morning again, already. I walk the ice back to the edge of the forest as the sun peeks over the eastern lakeshore. A beaver channel takes me quietly to a deadfall below an upland beaver pond. Water trickling down the slope from the dam adds a soft rhythm to the sound of the lake ice groaning and cracking in the fifteen-degree temperature. I wait a long half-hour for good light and ease farther into woods.

There's a hillside here that I call "The Park." By some quirk of nature, no hazel or dogwood brush is growing under the mature white oak, silver maple, and aspen. The thin covering of snow allows a view of at least a hundred yards in most directions and an oak deadfall provides a comfortable seat. The first hour passes quickly with red and gray squirrels providing entertainment with their late season gymnastics, struggling to get the last seeds from the ash and ironwood trees.

Then deer come crunching in from the north, brown shapes flickering through gaps in the brush. No antlers are showing but even a doe still gets my heart working hard. A big one leads this group of four. She follows the edge of the swamp and pauses behind two aspen trees fifty yards downslope. One more step and I can shoot. I have the gun in position, steady on the deadfall, the hammer at full cock, and my finger on the trigger.

She listens to the noises of the woods, the squirrels, the chickadees, and the nuthatches. Then she turns in a circle like a dog and lays down. The others follow her lead further back in the brush. I can see her head and neck for the next half-hour as she watches the squirrels, listens to the blue jays scold her, and continues with another day of her life in the forest. I lower the gun and wait.

I'm a patient man, but I'm not dressed for this

standoff. The cold slowly seeps in and forces me to make the first move. I slide right along the deadfall and line up the barrel for a shot between the aspen trees. The hammer drops, the gun booms out over the hillside and my view is absolutely obscured by the cloud of blue-gray smoke. When it clears, the deer remains in her bed, ears alert, trying to figure out what just happened.

I reload with shaking hands, pulling one of my pre-loaded cardboard tubes from a pocket, dumping the powder in, shaking the barrel to settle it, and clumsily ramming a ball down on top. The deer finally reacts as I thumb a percussion cap down on the nipple. She stands and gives me one more shot through the gap in the trees. I get results this time. She bounds away, tail flying high as the shot echoes through the woods, and another cloud of smoke adds its acrid smell to the atmosphere.

Where did the first shot go? I wish I knew. But I find one of the consequences of the second shot. A deep gash shines from the side of an ash tree ten yards upslope from the deer bed. I am usually a better shot that this. Today does not appear to be usual. I exit the woods to the lake, encouraged by the opportunity. I've missed easier shots at bigger deer and don't linger long on what could have been. Not yet anyway—the season is just starting. My cabin neighbor Tom is watching ice fishing tip-ups and enjoys the story with me. He too has missed deer.

Next weekend—Sunday morning. I leave home at an early six AM and head north. I can hunt today and Monday. Life is getting in the way of my recommitment. The dog is with me. She will hate me when she's left in the cabin but at least she will be there instead of moping around underfoot at home.

The sun is shining and the wind is blowing from the southwest when I unlock the cabin at midmorning. I decide to check out a clear-cut across the lake. The snow on the lake is again noisy as I backtrack my steps from last weekend. There's a trace of new white stuff, just enough to freshen tracks. A fisher has been actively circling the shore of the lake, probably the same one that stole a duck carcass from the cabin deck back in October. The tracks converge on an ice-level hole in the lake bank. I step up to it cautiously, concentrating my attention on the opening. A grouse chooses this moment to explode into the air right in front of my face and scare the hell out of me.

With my blood adrenaline level renewed, I continue on and cross deer tracks heading across the ice to an island. The evenly spaced straight set of tracks reminds me of the small eight-pointer that swam the same route several years ago. I paddled the canoe nearby, struggling to restrain my old Labrador from attempting to fetch it.

Up the lake bank and onto the logging trail. There's good news in the form of several fresh sets of tracks of various sizes. A skidding trail takes me in to a year-old clear-cut. A bear bait sign leftover from September is still tacked to a tree with an old rag fluttering in the wind above it. Just to the east is a three-sided wood tree stand with several cans and bottles littering the ground below. I can't fault this guy's choice of spots, on a beautiful pine ridge overlooking the clear-cut and several wetlands. I just wish he would have cleaned up after himself. I will once again be leaving the woods with more junk than I brought.

The woods have started to darken with only fifteen or twenty minutes of shooting time left. A well-used trail catches my eye. I follow it into the woods and lean against a pine high above a brushy valley. As it grows darker, I hear at least two separate animals moving towards me below the ridge. Deer?

Twigs are breaking and snow is crunching with the weight of more than a late-moving squirrel or grouse. But they are too far downslope for me to see and they are taking their time getting closer. Frustration grows as I stand motionless but can't make out their shapes. I finally make a move. One small step forward may be enough to see what's downslope. This one small step brings a snort from less than twenty yards to my right and a deer whirling away, crashing off into the dark brush. At least one other follows. Sneaky little devils . . .

Monday. Monday morning dawns with me trying tactics from the weekend before. I cross the lake and do my best to quietly get back into The Park. It's windy but sunny and nicely warm for this time of year. Lots of squirrels, chickadees, blue jays, and three ravens making strange noises and doing aerial acrobatics above. But no deer this time.

The afternoon will be my last chance for a deer. After lunch, a game of fetch with the dog, and packing the truck, I try hunting close to the cabin in spite of the lack of sign last weekend. Unlike the weekend before, there are fresh tracks. I spend the afternoon watching an oak grove, hoping at least one of those deer will take an afternoon walk in the sunshine. That doesn't work. So it's time to take action, time to try to find them, tiptoeing down an old logging trail with an hour left of daylight. A fat, tasty-looking grouse clucks at me from a beaver stump only ten yards away, tempting me to try to pick the fool off. But a shot will alert any deer. I continue on, hoping to be rewarded for my reserve.

I peer around a bend and stare at a shape that looks out of place. Before I can recognize it as the face of a deer staring back at me, another blows a whistling snort from the brush only yards down the trail. A mature doe bounds out and hightails it away down the trail.

The photographer-trained portion of my brain takes a snapshot and prints it. Her tail, amazingly large and amazingly white, unfurled, individual hairs spread, flying like a wild flag behind her.

A better man would not have shot, especially carrying a muzzleloader. But surprise, instinct, and the sheer proximity of the deer overrides what good senses I have. The gun comes to my shoulder and just as quickly booms out a cloud of gray smoke down the narrow tunnel-like confines of the logging trail. Of course it's a miss. High, well over her back, just like always happens when I take a quick running shot without thinking.

The lingering echoes and the black powder smoke leave me standing in the snow of the logging trail, somewhat shaken, my heart having hit two hundred miles an hour in a millisecond, knowing this year's season is fading with the setting sun and the sound of two deer crashing away.

Now is the time to think of what could have been. I did, after all, want to shoot a deer. I wanted to feel the adrenaline and excitement as I approached a still form down in the snow. I wanted to feel the warmth and smoothness of that gray-brown fur and enjoy the subtle beauty of the animal, even though it is dead and I have killed it. I wanted to warm my cold hands with its blood as I prepared it for the trip from the woods. I wanted to bask in the satisfaction that comes from a difficult task well done. And, yes, to even ponder the morality of what I had just done.

"All that" will have to wait until next year now. However, I did get most of what I came for. A unique experience. Adventure. Respect for the whitetail deer. New stories for next year's deer camp. And a reminder of my shortcomings. I head down the trail in the dimming daylight, crunching through the snow, knowing I'll be back next year.

FREE ADVICE and
LESSONS LEARNED

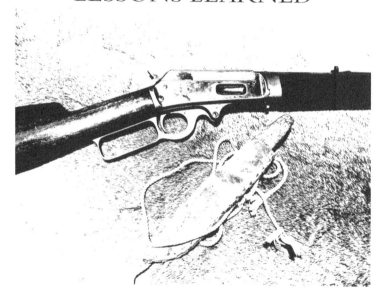

The Worst Guns Ever

If you subscribe to any print outdoor magazine, social media news feed, or outdoor blog these days, you get plenty of thinly veiled advertising and pompous opinions from outdoor writers on "The Best New Guns of the Year," "The Best Guns of the 20th Century," and "The Top Ten Guns for Deer Hunters." This list of lists could go on and on. What you won't get from these guys and gals is a comparable list of the worst guns ever produced, the worst gun for deer hunters or anything like that. Apparently these media outlets, some of them in existence for over a hundred years, are afraid of offending both advertisers and consumers. Well, what have I got to lose?

So here's one man's humble opinion of the Worst Guns Ever—at least in my fifty-some years of experience. And I ain't afraid of naming names . . .

Number Five
The Savage 99 lever-action rifle

Wow. I can hear the howls of outrage way off here in my remote bunker. This gun often makes lists like "The Top Ten Guns of the 20th Century" or most certainly "The Top Ten Lever-Action Deer Rifles." And in all honesty, some newer models of it should be on those lists. So I'll give it a break and call it only Number Five.

Hunting Around

It debuted over a hundred years ago with some very innovative features—like a rotary magazine, no exposed thumb hammer, and some pretty hot ammo for the day. Current writers still sing its praises, but seem to overlook the flaws I found in mine. My uncle Fred found me an old well-used 99 and sold it to me cheap back around in 1968. It was already over fifty years old by that time but I was thrilled to have it. No more carrying around a single-shot shotgun loaded with a single slug when we made the yearly deer hunt "Up North." I bagged my first buck with it, so you would think the romance of it would have lived on. Nope.

This old model was chambered in .30-30. Perhaps the most iconic deer round in history. But it also had a short barrel and a straight grip stock. You had better be holding on tight when the trigger was pulled. You should be wearing ear plugs, too. The recoil and the muzzle blast undoubtedly caused the severe flinch I still can have whenever I fire most any gun.

The safety was also a problem. While newer models had a handy thumb safety ergonomically located on the receiver, this early model had a little sliding lever down near the trigger guard. Try and find that tiny little lever when hunting in the cold Northwoods with cold hands and thick gloves. It was a very safe safety. For the deer. It cost me a shot at what still is the biggest deer I've ever seen.

I was walking the edge of a pine tree plantation in the midst of a heavy snowfall, head down, looking for sign when a large, very fresh deer track appeared in front of my insulated boot. I looked up and noticed a very large, very fresh buck with a body the size of a cow and antlers like an elk, calmly walking up the hillside maybe fifty yards away. I shouldered the 99 and slid that little safety backward with my cold gloved finger and reached for the trigger. The glove caught the little sliding safety and moved it back to "SAFE." I slid it back again and once again reached for the trigger. The buck picked up a little speed, headed for some thick cover in the side-wise blowing snowflakes. The glove caught the safety lever again and moved it to the wrong position for this situation.

That buck disappeared with me standing there flicking the safety back and forth. Not a shot was fired.

That was not the last deer that had the fortune of stumbling across me and the 99. I can honestly say it saved the lives of more deer than it took. I probably killed more grouse with it than deer. Give me dumb grouse clucking from a beaver stump in the Northwoods during deer season and I would gladly pick the head off it with that old .30-30. At least I got something to eat.

I eventually sold what could have been a family heirloom and moved on. The more I ponder this, that gun might deserve a place on the list closer to the real worst gun ever. Let me think about that while we continue.

Number Four
The Winchester Model 37
Single-shot 20-gauge shotgun

Yes, I once again hear more howls and outrage at

the choice of a historic American gun maker and a solid well-made gun that was the first gun of many younger old guys like me.

It was in fact my first real firearm if you don't count all the Daisy BB guns that I wore out in my early years. I bagged my first duck, my first pheasant, and my first rabbit with it. I carried it on my first deer hunt. I still own mine, which once again was a cheap buy from my Uncle Fred. I'm pretty sure the year was 1965 when I turned twelve and could legally hunt after taking the Firearms Safety Class. The Model 37 is a solid piece of American steel and walnut. It doesn't look bad and is still worth pretty good money on the used gun market. But I have my reasons for hating it.

The allure of the classic single-shot—"one shot, one kill"—soon wore off as I gained experience. I yearned for the fire power of the semi-automatic 12-gauge carried by an uncle while pheasant hunting at his farm. I liked the classic look and the two shots of my Uncle Fred's little double-barrel .410. I would have even settled for the slow but multiple shot capacity of my dad's clunky bolt-action 12-gauge. How many times did I watch in frustration as a pheasant flushed or a duck decoyed, only to fly away laughing as I missed with my one and only shot?

It had some mechanical issues too, even forgetting that it was a single-shot. This one was a "Youth Model" with a shortened stock for small kids. It didn't take me long to outgrow that. However, financial issues prevented me from moving up to an adult gun. The short stock meant that unless I really concentrated, most shots went high and over the head of the target. And what kid really concentrates much in the heat of the hunt? I missed a lot.

Then there were the safety issues—both mechanical and human. This was again an early model of the gun that Winchester did improve over the years. The mechanical safety consisted of a small exposed hammer that barely cleared the gun and had one hell of a strong spring behind it. More than one rooster pheasant came flushing up out of the grass, cackling with defiance as he flew away while I struggled to get the hammer back. So I adapted to the situation. If near the end of a cornfield, a place where the pheasants were likely to be concentrated, I was known to pull back the hammer and walk the last few yards cocked and loaded, ready for action. That's not an ideal situation if you happened to trip over a bent cornstalk or a rooster rises up from between your legs and scares the crap out of you and your trigger finger.

Number Three
The Hopkins & Allen
Single-Shot 16-Gauge

Now here's a gun I never even wanted but ended up spending hard-earned paper route money on anyway. Call it peer pressure. Or not wanting to offend one of your heroes. Or maybe a combination of those. After a few years of struggling with that aforementioned 20-gauge, I mentioned to Uncle Fred that I was ready to move up from a 20-gauge, ready to shoot a man's gun.

"I've got just the gun for you," he said, and offered

up a 16-gauge single-shot by the historic—and probably by then out of business—Hopkins & Allen.

It was hate—or at least "didn't like"—at first sight. It was a turn-of-the-century piece, and by that I mean 1900, and looked like it. Rode hard, put away wet. Well-abused. Somewhat rusty and sporting an ugly linseed oil finish. I had something more like a multi-shot pump gun in mind. But I meekly purchased the gun, for a cheap $15 if I remember right, because I didn't want to risk offending Uncle Fred. In retrospect, I think he was trying to teach me a few things. Like not being afraid to politely speak my mind and that big and fancy isn't always better.

I grew to hate that gun with a passion even after learning some basic gun repair techniques by stripping the finish off both wood and metal and refurbishing it into a decent-looking antique. But once again I struggled with the exposed hammer and the lack of more than one shot. Ammo was also a problem. Hunters had already started to turn away from the 16-gauge as too big for things that a 20-gauge could handle and too small for game that needed the power of a 12-gauge.

Perhaps the climatic event in our relationship was a goose hunt in the late 1960s. I huddled on the shore of a local lake, cold and miserable in fog and light rain, hoping for a goose to straggle by. Across the lake there came the sudden alarmed honking of a large flock of snow geese as they lifted off from the stubble of a picked corn field. As they gained altitude, geese started crumpling and falling from the sky, followed by the booming echo of numerous shotgun blasts rolling across the lake through the fog.

I watched the geese falling, shivered with excitement in the damp cold, and waited eagerly as the survivors came across the lake, straining to gain altitude. They came right over me, seemingly at treetop level, fighting the wind and rain while honking their fool heads off. I banged off three shots as fast as I could break open the single-shot, rip the spent shell out, and fumble in a new one.

Not a goose fell. I remember standing there, cold and wet as hell, shaking from the experience, and imagining the hunters across the lake laughing at me as they collected fallen geese. You can argue whether the gun, the situation, or my bad shooting was to blame. Whatever. I never forgave that gun and sold it for parts years later.

Number 2
High Standard Semi-automatic
12-Gauge Shotgun

I'm going to skip forward in time just a bit to get to this one. I'll elaborate more once I get to number one.

Back in the fall of 1975, a friend and I were working construction in a northern Minnesota town. Like many Northwoods contractors, we spent more time hunting and fishing than working. That's not meant to be a knock on Northwoods contractors and their work ethic. It is merely a statement of fact that largely holds true today. After all, grouse season was only open for a couple of months back in those days and only for about a hundred days now. You can work the other three hundred or so days. Sick of my current shotgun (see "Worst Gun Ever" coming up soon) and having some money earned on days when we did work, I walked into a local hardware store to purchase a cheap 12-gauge pump that was on sale.

Right next to the pump gun was a shiny new "High Standard" semi-auto 12-gauge. It was on sale too, actually cheaper than the pump gun, and it had a more open modified choke. It was obviously the better choice for grouse, maybe better for decoying ducks, and the thought of a semi-auto after all those single-shots tipped the balance. I walked out of the store with it. I should have bought several cases of shotgun shells while there.

The gun was a pretty solid gun, at least to begin with. But there were problems. The user's manual proudly proclaimed that the gun, with its state-of-the-art gas operating system, was capable of firing five shots in one second. I think they actually underestimated this capability by a wide margin. I firmly believe there were times when a grouse would flush and suddenly five loads of shot would be going down the barrel at the same time.

Branches would fall from the sky, blown clean from their parent tree. Small trees would tip over with shattered trunks. Other hunters and dogs would cower in surprise and fear from the volleys I let loose. Few grouse or other game succumbed. I was just not yet ready in my journey as a hunter to handle the responsibility of all that fire power.

Perhaps due to this abuse, the gun also developed a very irritating mechanical flaw. Pull the trigger once and miss, pull the trigger again and nothing would happen. I would look to the gun and find one shell jammed in the loading ramp and another laying at my feet. Thus I ended up where I had begun, where I was trying to get away from. I was shooting a semi-automatic single-shot.

The only good thing gained from this experience was the trade value of that gun. I swapped it for a slightly used Savage Fox double-barrel and moved on, pretty much sticking with double-barrels even as I write this almost fifty years later.

So, time for that drum roll and what we've all been waiting for!

The Number One, By Far
Extremely Worst Gun Ever
12-gauge Single-shot of Japanese manufacture

I'm not trying to be kind here or duck any hateful comments. I just can't honestly remember the actual name brand (and I use that term very lightly) of this shotgun. I do remember it was produced in Japan by a company whose name started with an "S." It cost $24 dollars in the fall of 1971 at a local discount store in Bemidji, Minnesota. It was chosen partially because of the "price point" but also because it had a modified choke while all other affordable brands had full chokes. Being a poor college student with limited funds and equipment, I was trying to make the most of the situation. The forests surrounding the city and college were teeming with grouse. An open-choked cheap shotgun and some inexpensive low-based shells were all that were needed to take advantage of that situation.

Hunting Around

I should have realized what I was purchasing. There were warning flags. The fact that I never heard of the company should have been one. But the most obvious question should have been quality. Left unsupervised by store personnel, my roommate and I had to disassemble three of the guns in the store's stock to get one that would function. We took the stock and receiver from one, added the barrel from another, and finally snapped on the forearm from yet one more. At the end of this project, the gun opened and shut and stayed together like it should. I paid up and we slunk out of the store before some store clerk wised up.

I became a grouse-hunting legend over the next four years of my academic career. While the gun had "modified choke" stamped on it, in reality it was more an open-cylinder, perhaps blunderbuss choke. It sprayed out number 7½-shot from gas station-purchased shot-shells with a pattern wider than a bus. There was no problem hitting the broadside of a barn or a grouse. They didn't have a chance.

It actually got to the point where my hunting partners would call me over when they had flushed a grouse and missed. We'd move ahead for a re-flush and that unfortunate grouse would go down in flames. I say that because the grouse was likely to be roasted over a hastily prepared campfire within minutes of its demise. We were literally starving college students in those days and we had to choose between food or beer with our meager funds.

So why did I come to hate, with the utmost

passion, a gun I became a living legend with?

This gun turned out to be a lesson in "quality" and a lesson in "diversity." Let's tackle "diversity" first. It did fell more than its share of grouse. I even bagged my first ever five-bird limit with it on one sunny fall day in 1974. I remember that day well. But it was next to worthless at the longer ranges needed for ducks, geese, and pheasants.

I didn't get many chances at those birds back in the day. The few chances I had were lessons in frustration as I got off my one and only shot at a pheasant or tried to pass shoot at ducks forty yards out. They easily flew through the gaping holes in that shot pattern.

But what really brought this gun to the top was "quality," a word I use with much sarcasm. I should add a qualifier and say "lack of quality." After a couple seasons of use, something happened within the chamber of that cheap gun. The precious inexpensive low brass shells I could afford started sticking in the chamber, unmoved by the ejector. I found that the problem was somewhat less if I used high brass shells of a well-known name-brand. But what broke college student can afford those without cutting into the beer budget?

This reached the heights of insanity in the last autumn I spent as a hunting student. If you met me, you might remember it. Picture me in my early twenties, dressed in less than classic upland shooting clothes, wandering the forest carrying a cheap-looking single-shot. Nothing weird about that, you might say. But what about the arrow I was carrying, snugged up against the barrel of that gun?

Yes, that was what I stooped to. Unable to afford trading the gun, I wandered the grouse woods carrying a tip-less arrow, ready to ram it down the barrel of that POS gun to eject a spent shell, maybe in time to reload and get a shot at a second stupid grouse. In my defense, it was an innovative adaptation that meant I didn't have to look around for a straight stick to poke down the barrel while a grouse clucked from a stump yards away.

It might have also been the start of my current obsession with muzzleloading smoothbore shotguns. I don't feel all that challenged. I can load a muzzleloader just as fast as I could poke a stuck shell out of that old 12-gauge. I had a lot of practice.

So there you have it. The raw truth about five guns that could have been better. In some cases, a lot better! I realize I might have stepped on a few toes of those types that like to wax nostalgic about the good old days. They remember that special long package under a Christmas tree way back when. Or the day a grandfather or a well-loved relative handed them down a piece of family history. Or a gun they wished they had never sold. But truth be told, when it comes to my gun collection, the good old days are now!

The Best Knife for the
Bush Big Game Hunt

The Best Knife for the Bush Big Game Hunt

Now you might think the title for this story is strange. I do too. Most readers probably wonder what a "Bush Big Game Hunt" is. Here's the deal: the story itself came about in a strange way that needs some explanation.

I currently market myself as a "semi-famous, award-winning author." After all, I do have some fans that recognize my name and my writing has won numerous awards. Notice I didn't include "expert" in that title. However, it seems that some folks do consider you an expert once you publish stories, write books, win awards, and claim to be semi-famous. Guys like my friend Jerry.

Jerry is a writer of some note himself. But he makes no claims to being an outdoor sports writer. Thus when he was contacted by a guy who wanted an expert outdoor writer to assist in writing a new blog, Jerry passed him off on me.

The would-be blog guy told me he was looking for writers to provide informational articles on "bush craft." I kinda scratched my head and had him explain further. "Bush craft" is apparently another name for what I would simply call "survival skills." Things like knowing how to build a fire by rubbing two sticks together, making a shelter out of a tarp, and eating bugs. Things that you need to know and do if stranded in some remote scary place. I initially deferred. I didn't really consider myself an expert in this area and, besides, the guy wanted me to write for free. Being already "semi-famous," I usually don't write for free unless it's for a charity or a worthy cause. But the guy persisted. He liked that I was a big game hunter and thought I might have useful information for potential blog subscribers. He finally offered me a hundred bucks to write a piece about The Best Knife for the Bush Big Game Hunt. "What if you could only carry one knife on a hunt?" he asked. "Write me a story about that knife."

Okay, I've tried plenty of knives while hunting, lost most of them, and moved on to another one. So maybe I could do this. So I did. See what you think and I'll get back to you after the end.

By the time daylight arrived, snow was blowing horizontally across the foothills of Wyoming's Big Horn Mountains and right into my face. But there was enough visibility to identify a small herd of pronghorn antelope, bedded down a half-mile away on the lee side of a butte. I got hiking and approached downwind and out of sight before dropping off my backpack and sneaking across the windy top of the butte.

Things had changed in the half-hour stalk. The antelope had left their cozy beds and were long gone. Where? Maybe just over the next ridge. Nope. Maybe just over the next ridge. No again.

Finally there they were, over the next of several more ridges, grazing as the snow flew past. That's how I ended up miles from camp and over a mile from my well-provisioned backpack with a buck antelope in the sights of my 6.5 mm Husqvarna Mauser. The gun did its job. Now the work began in the field dressing of the buck to cool and preserve that wonderful meat.

The Best Knife for the Bush Big Game Hunt

My back pack was still a mile away. In it was my favorite knife, a classic Western brand sheath knife. One I had purchased some twenty years before and was still my go-to knife for these off-the-road excursions. The 5-inch blade wasn't stainless, the handle was old-fashioned stacked leather, and the sheath had a funky-looking oak leaf design embossed on it. But it was everything needed in a situation like this—a hefty blade with a good edge that could cut through hide and rib bones. And while I hate to admit this type of brutal behavior, experience had shown it was tough enough to withstand beating with a rock if a bone needed breaking.

But that knife was a long ways away. What I did have was a knife that is never far away when I am outside the bounds of citified civilization. A Wenger Swiss army knife purchased in Zurich, Switzerland, in 1987 and monogrammed with my first name. This was the handy compact Hiker model, complete with one blade, corkscrew, can opener, screwdriver, saw blade, and a few others. It could peel an apple, cut kindling, open a can of beans, pop the cork on a wine bottle, or tighten a gun screw. In this case, it could also field dress an antelope.

Strangely enough, I have harvested two other antelope since that day when that Swiss army knife happened to be the only one available. When I get to chasing antelope, I end up traveling farther than planned and lighter than planned.

I don't recommend the Swiss army knife as the best knife or the only knife to carry when miles from a road and a dirty job needs to be done. There are better choices. These knives need to be handy to carry and with a more comfortable sheath than the stiff one that Western knife came with. That way it will be on my hip instead of in a backpack miles away. It needs to be durable and big enough for the job. And it can't cost so much that I will lose sleep when it gets "misplaced." Because that just might happen.

I haven't been back to Wyoming for antelope for many years. Since then I have switched to Montana and mostly solo hunt off the grid where no cell phone can ring or vibrate. I also tend to target bigger animals like mule deer and elk, farther off the road, and a long ways out in the bush. In this situation I don't think you can go wrong with a fixed-blade knife with a hefty four- to six-inch blade and a sheath that will stick on your hip without getting in the way. I have learned not to let that knife out of my sight.

If the elk I'm looking for shows up and goes down, the Swiss army knife isn't going to be up to the job. Elk are two, three, or four times the size of an average deer or antelope. The hide on them is also two, three, or four times tougher. However, they can be boned out without ruining the edge on the right knife.

I no longer bang on the back of a knife to break bones. Boning out means separating meat from hide and bone. It can be done without hacking any edge-dulling bones and with a minimum of hide cutting. I currently carry a J. Marttiini Lynx from Kellam Knives.

This one has a 4 ½-inch forged stainless steel blade and a classic birch wood handle. I picked it up for $60 at a silent auction fund raiser hosted by a group of men of Finnish heritage. One of them told me the knife was a classic "puukko," or in his words—"the everyday workhorse knife all hard-working Finns carry at all *times." Kellam's website confirms this information and lists the Lynx and other models in an assortment of handles, blades, and sheaths starting at about $70.*

Cost is something most of us have to consider when choosing an everyday bush knife. I have nothing against collectors and others who are willing to spend hundreds, even thousands, of dollars on handmade, one-of-a-kind, artisanal metal knives. But does that knife belong in the bush, hacking kindling, dissecting large animals, opening cans, and being used as a fire striker? What if it gets misplaced?

That classic Western knife I mentioned earlier now resides somewhere along the banks of the Missouri River in central Montana. It fell from a backpack compartment left unzipped while distracted with packing out a deer. Others have been lost in similar ways and not just by me. I have found two knives that other outdoorsmen lost. Ideas on what the definition of quality is will vary. I think there are knives, like my Marttiini, that provide both value and quality at less than a hundred dollars.

I do sometimes carry folding knives—lock-back knives with big single blades. But only as backup knives. I currently own ones manufactured by Gerber, Colombia River Knife & Tool (CRKT), and Buck Knives.

However, I am leery of them when the going gets tough. I have had one fail with a broken blade and one with a broken locking mechanism. Perhaps it was my rough handling at the time or my "cheap" budget. But they failed where fixed blades haven't. I am trying out the newer replaceable-blade folding knives made by Havalon. So far they are an asset with skinning and meat-boning tasks but the super-sharp, thin blades limit their practical functions if you do have to take on some bone.

So if someone asks me "what's the one knife I won't part with if stuck in the badlands of Montana," I'll stick with my current Marttiini puukko or a similar sturdy fixed-blade with a comfortable sheath. I will survive just fine.

However, I might just try and sneak a Wenger or Victorinox Swiss army knife into a pocket while nobody's looking, just in case. The best knife for the bush big game will be the one you are actually carrying when you need it.

There you have it. Expert advice on knife selection. But there's more to the story. I emailed this piece off to the would-be blog guy. He loved it and asked where to send the money. That was the last I heard of him. Further emails went unanswered and the hundred bucks he promised never showed up.

So take this advice for what it's apparently worth. Or send me some money if it really works for you.

After the Shot

.

After the Shot

Sometime over fifty years ago, I was standing beneath a huge cottonwood tree, basking in the November sun when my father's 12-gauge boomed several times. A shot at any deer was a case for excitement in those days. We got one day, and one day only, to hunt deer in western Minnesota farm country. You had to make the most of any opportunity. I abandoned my post and crashed through one hundred yards of thick Minnesota River bottomland brush towards the action.

Dad was standing near a fallen tree, excited about what had just happened. "Three or four deer came by and stopped right here—I'm sure I hit one," he said. "It turned around and ran back east."

While he stood at the point of the shot, I walked back along the transition zone of woods and cattails marking the floodplain swamp. It didn't take many steps to find sign that even an amateur tracker like me could follow. Cattails sprayed brilliant red, still wet in the afternoon sun. I hurried down the trail and found a big whitetail doe crashed dead into the thick stuff. That was my first deer trailing experience. An easy one with a happy ending.

Things haven't been always as simple as that sunny day in the Minnesota River bottoms. I've hunted and taken deer in four states. Make that five if you count the fork horn buck that bounced off the truck bumper during a duck hunt in North Dakota. Many lessons in tracking have been learned from all those experiences. However, one really stands out whenever I end up on a difficult trail.

I was hunting a big chunk of Minnesota forest with a mixed group of friends and strangers. One guy got a shot at a big buck and was sure he connected. We found hair, bone, and blood at the site. But we quickly lost the trail as five or six hunters circled around, stirring up the area and destroying clues. Then one guy stepped in and took charge.

Smokey was a tall, soft-spoken Native American who spent most of his time in the woods. I didn't know him well. Others in the party did and immediately stopped their wandering around and listened to his advice.

"We've got too many people here," he said.

He then handed out instructions, directing everyone but me to circle ahead in the distance and take up specific posts at places he knew a wounded deer might pass. Once the other hunters had a head start, he looked to me. "Let me do the trailing. Stay back and off to one side. Now we're going to get this deer."

I'm not sure why Smokey picked me to hang with him. But the next hour was spent learning from a master. Smokey moved ahead deliberately, finding the spot where the buck had crossed an open meadow, leaving hair and just a speck of blood as it ducked under a tall fence and into the trees. I followed close behind as he quietly pointed out what he was looking for and finding.

After the Shot

A scuff mark of dried dead leaves turned up and showing their darker moist underside. Bits of white belly hair, fat, and blood high on brush where the deer pushed through. A small bone fragment in another spot. A splatter of individual blood drops scattered in the middle of the trail where the deer had paused for a moment.

He pieced these clues together one bit at a time. "This deer is hit low through the brisket and a leg. It'll be bedded down soon. Either we get it when it jumps or one of the other guys will have a chance when it runs."

He was right on all accounts. We jumped the deer in thick cover and didn't get a shot. But it ran right where Smokey predicted and the hunter that made the initial shot finished what he had started. The deer, a beautiful eleven-point buck, had been hit low through the brisket and had a broken front leg.

Not every hunter can have a learning experience like that which includes on-the-spot mentoring from a real expert. But there are things I believe can up the odds the next time a deer doesn't go down in its tracks right after the trigger is pulled.

For starters, if you are hunting in the thick stuff, follow that old advice and "use enough gun." Nothing leaves a good blood trail like a big exit wound from a 140-grain or better bullet. I'm not here to argue about the perfect gun or the best deer caliber. That friendly discussion will hopefully go on around deer campfires and kitchen tables for many years to come.

I recently had one of those friendly discussions

with an outdoor expert who was praising 6 mm/.24-calibers as deer guns. I weighed in with a recent experience where a 100-grain .243 bullet failed to exit a large doe that was hit broadside through the lungs at fifty yards. It died quickly but left no blood trail or other sign in thick cover. We were lucky to find it.

While some would argue the bullet had performed perfectly by expending all its energy and humanely killing the deer, I like an exit hole and a blood trail. Especially when hunting in thick brush, cattail swamps, and other types of cover where a deer disappears after the shot. The tiny entrance hole made by a 100-grain bullet can easily plug on the big, fat, hairy, tough whitetails found in northern-tier states. My favorite is the 6.5x55 Mauser with a 140-grain bullet. But there are plenty of other good choices to discuss around those campfires and kitchen tables.

Second, share your experiences and ask other hunters about theirs, especially when hanging out with new or younger hunters. Tell others what you saw and didn't see. How did the deer react after the shot? What did you find for sign? How far did the deer go?

One other practice can give you tracking experience even if a deer drops within sight or was easy to track. Enjoy the excitement of harvesting that deer. Show it respect and take care of the field dressing. While doing that, note the path of the bullet through the deer and the organs it touched. Then follow the trail back to the site of the bullet's impact. Look at the path the deer picked through cover after being hit. What hair, bone, blood or other sign do you find? The deer may be down but lessons can be learned and experience gained for the next time.

Many of these personal lessons got put into use last November on another sunny afternoon. I was seated in an elevated box stand in a northern Minnesota pine plantation. The last day of the season was winding down and the weather was unseasonably warm. That meant no snow for tracking, limited deer movement, and any deer that was shot had to be dealt with right away instead of aging on the meat pole. Nothing was moving past my stand except the same red squirrel that had been scurrying around, scolding me all afternoon. Then, like often happens, I felt the need to swivel in the chair and check behind. There, standing in a small clearing forty yards away, was the six-pointer, sunlight reflecting off his small rack.

I say "the" six-pointer, not "a" six-pointer because I recognized this one. He had posed for our trail cameras over the past three months and once scared the heck out of me with a snort while walking into a bear bait station on a dark morning. He wasn't what many hunters would call a trophy. However, the sun was setting on the last day of the season and he was available.

I swung the compact Ruger .44 Magnum carbine around and started to line up the sights. He stepped forward and disappeared into a patch of thick understory, brown-gray hide perfectly camouflaged in the brown-gray brush. I waited, finger on the trigger, heart pounding. A deer body moved into a small opening, framed between a big pine and scraggly birch clump. I pulled the trigger, sending a 240-grain hollow point on its way.

There was enough of an opening to see the deer kick its back legs, then spin and run. It also sent three or four other deer scattering from the scene with tails high, leaping logs, crashing off into the swamp to the west. I lost track of the target deer in the mess but got the general idea that it had headed downhill to the south at a dead run. I waited a few minutes, confident that the leg kick meant a solid body hit and the buck would be lying dead not far away.

I climbed down the ladder and used the stand as a landmark to the gap between the birch and the pine where the deer had stood. Right away there was lots of blood and scuffed leaves where the deer left at high speed. I marked the spot with a piece of flagging tape and looked for the next, finding and marking more spots downhill through the pines.

For the first fifty yards the spots were five to ten feet apart and big enough to allow leap frogging from one to the next. But then they thinned out. Soon I was stopping and starting, moving only a couple feet at a time while searching in the green moss and the rust brown leaves and pine needles.

As the obvious sign started to fade, I slowed down, looking for more than just blood. Things like scuffed leaves, hair, a game trail the deer might have followed, or broken brush. I dropped pieces of orange tracking tape wherever something was found, and kept looking back at the pattern of orange tape for ideas.

Perhaps thirty yards ahead of the last sign, I saw a

bloody smear shoulder-high on the trunk of an aspen. And there were more, headed in a straight line for the swamp. I moved ahead faster and spotted the horizontal white line of a deer belly stretched out in an opening. The deer was laid out in the pine needles, very much dead from a classic double-lung shot, but had managed to travel over two hundred yards before going down.

I knelt beside the deer, admired its sleek form, and paid my respects. Then I texted my sons the good news and got down to the field dressing. I had time to think while working, time to think about the tracking lessons this deer had reaffirmed.

I was also reminded of one other basic deer hunting lesson. The deer being field-dressed was not the six-pointer. He would be posing for our game cameras again. I had bagged a beautiful mature doe, who likely was being trailed by the buck. I had assumed there was just one deer and that the body that appeared in the gap between trees was the buck. I was wrong.

The doe was perfectly legal in this case and a welcome addition to the other wild game in the freezer. Still, it's a fact that I didn't know what I was shooting at. That's a lesson that won't be forgotten the next time my finger tightens on a trigger, before the next tracking job starts.

OUT WEST

In the Beginning

In the Beginning

All obsessions have a beginning. Some an event that triggers us to take action on a dream and then keeps us chasing that dream. Hunting the great expanses of the western states has become one of mine. The beginnings of that obsession are clear. November of 1975, to be more precise.

I was working with my former college roommate and good friend, trying to earn money for graduate school by following him around on construction projects and hammering nails where and when he told me. Kim was a hunting buddy too and shared my dreams about hunting "Out West." We decided to turn those dreams into action and trek to the Black Hills of South Dakota, hot on the trail of exotic mule deer instead of Minnesota whitetails. We knew nothing of the territory other than reports from friends and magazine articles. But we had guns, ammo, and some camping equipment. And we were young and stupid. So off we went.

As with many of these trips, the drive to the destination provided adventure even before we arrived. This was a low-budget, short trip. There were no funds for hotel stays and we had to get back to work before some homeowner wondered why we weren't showing up to complete his torn-apart home. There wasn't a lot of planning involved. We got home after working all day, threw a bunch of equipment into Kim's Dodge

Hunting Around

Ramcharger (an early SUV), picked up his life-long friend, Scott, and headed out for an all-night drive.

The early part of the drive went fine. Scott was the type of guy that always had a story about something and loved to tell it. In this case, he told us the entire plot of the Burt Reynold's movie *The Longest Yard*. And I mean the entire story, play by play in this case, since it involved a football game. But even Scott ran out of gas at some point and I was left behind the wheel of the Dodge, hurtling down the dark highways of rural South Dakota while the other two took a nap. I took a nap too and ended up driving down the ditch on the opposite side of the highway. I woke up before any real damage was done and jerked the truck back onto the road, waking Kim and Scott in the process. Nobody slept well after that . . .

We arrived in the famed "Hills" late in the morning and got down to hunting. Having no idea where to start, we simply drove down a road until numerous tracks in the fresh snow of the road ditch indicated that deer were around. Good enough!

The truck was parked and guns were loaded. I would be remiss in recounting this adventure if I didn't mention that Kim had discovered halfway through the drive that his gun was still back at home. It stood behind the front door of his house, forgotten in the haste to pack, sporting a brand-new telescopic sight that he had purchased specifically for this trip. It's a good thing Scott had packed a spare.

We spread out and headed up the mountain, our big western mule deer hunting trip now a reality, not just

In the Beginning

a dream.

Being young and in shape from all the ladder climbing involved in construction work, I reached the crest of a long upsloping ridge without much problem and started slowly working through the pine trees and snow. Less than an hour into the hunt, I saw movement and hunkered down to see what was up. A whitetail deer doe proceeded to walk past me following a well-used trail. She was soon followed by a medium-sized eight-point buck. Also a whitetail, just like we had back in Minnesota. I now know that the Black Hills has both mule deer and whitetails. But we were young and stupid back then.

This wasn't a time to be picky. It was time to shoulder my gun and take advantage of a buck deer standing thirty yards away. That's when buck fever hit. An affliction I've been susceptible to for many years and still have not been totally cured of. A moment later my ears were ringing from the five fast shots I'd let rip at that deer. And he was still running, somehow untouched by the barrage of lead from my old .30-30.

That was the only deer encounter on the first day. Back at the truck, Kim and Scott quizzed me on deer identification and had difficulty believing whitetails were roaming the pine trees of this semi-mountainous terrain. But more adventure was to come. We now had to survive a night out in the boonies, sleeping in the back of the SUV at near zero temperatures, in summer-weight sleeping bags.

Let's just say that we did survive and learned a lot. Like sleeping in the middle of the back of a truck, sharing the body heat of two other hunters, is better than being on the outside, jammed up against the cold metal of a wheel well.

We splurged for breakfast at a local small town café early the next morning, warming up with the friendly local people. Scott kept these regulars entertained with stories of the last day and the cold night. The cook even came out of the kitchen to hassle Scott about special-ordering hot oatmeal for breakfast. Apparently that was not a big seller in these parts. I'm pretty sure the locals talked about us after we left, maybe even called us young and stupid.

The hardships of the last night were soon forgotten. On our next foray up the mountain, Kim was watching two red squirrels fight over possession of a pine tree when another deer walked into view. A very nice ten-point whitetail buck. Like me, Kim didn't hesitate to take a shot. And he shot better. The only problem was that the deer ran several hundred yards down the opposite side of the mountain before expiring. The three of us gathered over the big beautiful buck, admired it at length, and then got to work. It now had to be transported back up over the mountain and down the other side to the truck.

These days I'm a little bit smarter and much older. I'd start slicing and dicing that deer on the spot and only haul out the usable parts. Head, hide, and meat in this case. But we were from Minnesota. Our deer-hunting culture teaches us to drag out the entire deer so it can be properly displayed to other hunters and neighbors. So we did. It took most of the day and left us exhausted and enjoying a celebratory beer back at the truck. Again I would be remiss in telling this story without mentioning that the next day we found a road to the other side of the mountain that came within a hundred yards of where that buck died. One guy could have slid it downhill to the truck, all by himself, in a couple minutes.

We hunted hard for another day and survived another cold night snuggled together in the truck. The next day I ended the afternoon by bagging a fork horn buck that chased a doe past me at close range. In this case he was close enough that even my buck fever couldn't save him. And I was able to slide him downhill to the road where Kim picked me up after dark. But that wasn't the end of the day's adventures.

Scott was missing. He hadn't shown up at the truck at the appointed time. We drove back into the mountains on the new road, stopping to beep the horn and call, hoping for a response. Well into the evening we got a shout back and found Scott. He was perched high in a big pine tree with his rifle on the ground, propped up against the trunk.

As Scott would tell the story, he was surrounded by a pack of hungry wolves, eyes shining in the dark, snarling and howling like werewolves in a cheap horror film. Rather than shoot it out with them, he climbed into the tree and stayed there until the truck's headlights sent them scurrying. Forget that only smaller, meeker coyotes, not wolves, lived in the Black Hills. "They had to be wolves," he claimed. "They were the size of German Shepherds!"

Like I said, Scott was a great story teller. And all great story tellers have vivid imaginations.

So we made our way back to Minnesota. Scott didn't get his deer but did get some great stories to pass on. Kim and I didn't get the giant exotic mule deer bucks we had been talking about while pounding nails and "planning" the trip. But we were young and stupid. And we had one hell of a great time.

Belle Fourche Harry

Belle Fourche Harry

The Belle Fourche River cuts a wide deep valley, winding through western South Dakota's rolling prairie. This isolated ranching country is straight out of the Old West with far-flung villages named Hereford, White Owl, and Elm Springs. It's also some of the best mule deer hunting territory east of Wyoming.

My father and I felt lucky to have drawn non-resident deer licenses for this area. But that was only half the battle. As lowly tourist hunters from Minnesota, we needed to find a hunting spot in this area of strictly private land where hunting privileges were usually reserved for friends, relatives, or high paying clients. So Dad, the fearless farmer-turned-insurance-agent, started knocking on ranch house doors, and kept knocking until he found Harry.

Harry looked like he belonged there. He was in his mid-sixties and as stout, weathered gray, and tough as the gnarled cottonwood trees lining the banks of the river. But he had no qualms about us strangers hunting his ranch. He welcomed us, helped set up our camper on a deserted farm site, and gave us the run of several thousands of acres of prime deer country.

We soon found out Harry was aptly named. It was early November and the ceaseless prairie winds were cold even for us natives of frigid Minnesota. Harry would show up every morning to milk the lone cow that mingled with the beef cattle in the corral. He milked the cow by hand, from a stool, dressed in only jeans and a flannel shirt while we stood by, bundled in our warmest hunting clothes. The plaid flannel shirt was always unbuttoned half down, with ample gray chest hair sprouting from it like the hide of a winter-toughened animal.

There were other things about Harry that fit the tough old rancher stereotype. Like his absolute hatred of coyotes. I watched one repeatedly tilt its head back and howl at the sunrise the first morning. I held my fire, content to observe this primeval scene and not disturb any nearby deer. When Harry rumbled up later in the morning in his old Ford pickup, I made the mistake of telling him, thinking he would enjoy reliving the moment with me. Instead he launched into an expletive-laced, anti-varmint tirade that lasted several minutes. It ended with an ultimatum.

He leaned out of the pickup window, finger pointing directly at me, and made things perfectly clear. "If you are going to hunt on my property, you will shoot and kill—or at least wound—every damn coyote you see!"

Ok, when in Rome . . .

I managed to shoot the next coyote I saw and got another lesson in life on the Dakota prairie. An elderly woman lived in an old homestead above the ravine where I was hunting. She walked down the fence line to meet me and called out down the hill—"I heard shots. Did you get your deer?"

"Nope," I yelled back. "Just a toothless old coyote." I lugged the scarred old male up the hill and instantly made a new friend.

"Thank you, thank you!" She literally danced with excitement, hopping from foot to foot on what had to be eighty-year-old legs, and finally hugging me. "That one's been eating my chickens every night! I can sleep again!"

I guess it's pretty hard to enjoy the lonesome howl of a coyote when you are worrying about the livestock that provides both your livelihood and the food on your table.

But things and people are often more complex than they at first seem. We soon learned that the more time you spent with Harry, the more you learned about the dangers of stereotypes and assumptions. He stopped by our campsite every evening, obviously hungry for company and conversation. We heard plenty of stories about the hard life of a South Dakota prairie and of his younger days in rough and tumble cow towns. But we also heard about his wife and family.

He married late in life to an older woman with what many men would consider too much baggage. A birth defect had left her with only one hand and she had a son from a previous marriage. The son had died ten years before, under suspicious circumstances, in the dark alley of a city hundreds of miles away. Harry still mourned and wondered why.

And if you were lucky enough to hang out with Harry and his wife, you soon learned a new definition of self-sufficiency. While neighboring ranchers were poisoning the grasshoppers plaguing their wheat fields, he cultivated habitat for sharp-tailed grouse and Hungarian partridge. These grasshopper-eating game birds were so numerous they got in the way—flushing loudly from thickets in the ravines of the river valley, spooking the deer we were quietly trying to stalk.

Lunch at his spacious but simple ranch house was home-canned venison cooked in thick gravy and poured over potatoes and vegetables from the garden. The milk came from that cow at our campsite, and the fresh baked bread was made from wheat he grew and personally ground to flour. The *Mother Earth News* or some survivalist-based journalist would have loved to interview Harry and his wife. However, I'm not sure they would have been flattered.

We never did get a deer on that trip too many years ago. We did spend a long week roaming the hills, collecting memories, and hanging out with Harry. Those memories now seem more important than any deer. I know Harry is long since gone and would not be there to welcome me back to his ranch. But I might head back to the Belle Fourche River country again sometime anyway. I know times have changed. But I'm thinking that where there was one Harry, there might be more.

Ten Lessons I Learned
in Montana

I really hadn't planned on deer hunting in Montana. I didn't expect to win the license lottery on my first try. So when the license appeared in the mail, there was a sudden realization that some serious planning was needed. After all, this was not going to be a full-service, guided walk in the woods. At the ripe old age of fifty-something, I was going to Montana alone.

I was tired of my hunting partners saying —"maybe next year . . ." This time no other person's schedule, family, or finances were holding me back. Of course, that also meant there would be no one else to lean on with a busted ankle, to loan me a spare gun should one of those break, or to help drag a dead deer over a mountain or through a valley. And having no partners to share expenses with meant living out of the back of my truck on the extremely low-budget plan.

I managed to survive the adventure and learned more in conquering Montana by myself than I would have on any group or guided hunt. Here's my top-ten list of lessons learned—just in case you are interested in trying this yourself.

1. Make sure you know
where your binoculars are

As it turned out, mine weren't at my lake cabin, waiting to be picked up on the way west. Backtracking

115

home would have cost me seven hours of drive time, another fifty dollars in gas, and excessive ridicule from my wife. The next available sporting goods store had a decent pair of 10x50s on sale. That's what credit cards are for.

2. Bring your credit card (see above)

The one with some credit left on it. Remember, your buddies aren't going to be there to bail you out like they've done a few times before.

3. Take along your own music

There are places on Highway 200 in central Montana, and many other places on the western frontier, where your radio will not find a station. If it does, you can have any kind of music you want—as long as it's Country.

4. Never pass a Montana gas station without checking your gauge

Perhaps better yet, never pass a Montana gas station without topping off the tank! Halfway between Glendive and Jordan, at five o'clock on a Sunday morning, my hair turned several shades grayer when I looked at the gas gauge. Let me warn you, where there is no radio reception, there are no gas stations. And remember some cash too, in addition to the credit card mentioned in #2. There still are wild and unspoiled places where cash is needed to purchase fuel.

5. Keep your mouth shut in small town cafés

I grew up in small towns and should have seen this

one coming. I was waiting for my breakfast sandwich in a small town café, listening to an elderly gentleman who was loudly holding court at the head of a tableful of regulars. I innocently asked if he had heard the weather forecast for the next few days. I fell right into his tourist trap. "Hell, no!" he announced to the whole establishment. "Only a damn fool would try to predict the weather in MONTANA!!!!"

6. Things will go bump in the night

I camped at a primitive public campground the first night, many miles out in the boondocks. Mice and assorted larger vermin kept me awake, scrounging through the campsite and actually jumping against the truck, hoping for the easy pickings they had experienced with summer tourists. The last straw was the mouse that ran across my face sometime after midnight. It probably didn't help that it was Halloween and I was the only camper to visit for trick or treating.

7. Take along your sense of adventure

I could have brought along the scoped, deadly accurate 6.5X55 Husqvarna Mauser rifle I normally use for deer hunting. But as that old guy at the café would say —"Any damn fool can shoot a deer in MONTANA!!!" The hunt became an adventure by carrying a single-shot, peep-sighted rifle shooting slow 38-55 cartridges just like the old cowboys. Several mule deer bucks don't realize this decision probably saved their furry white butts.

8. A GPS will tell you both good news and bad news

I tried an experiment once I finally shot a deer. With the deer's location safely entered in my GPS, I hiked back to the truck, dropped off all unnecessary gear, and tried to return using only landmarks. A lone bald eagle, perched in a cottonwood tree hundreds of yards from my landmarks, made me stop and check the electronic gizmo. It pointed straight to the eagle, who was apparently contemplating a brunch of fresh deer liver. The GPS led me directly back to the deer.

That's the good news. Now the bad news. The GPS told me I had a half-mile, give or take thirty feet, to drag one dead deer, all by myself.

9. Remember your sense of hospitality

I forgot mine. I didn't offer a lone hunter from Washington a cup of coffee when I had plenty and could make more. He could have been a useful contact for future adventures in another great hunting and fishing state. But I got greedy and fed him bad information in hopes that he wouldn't head off towards a mulie buck I had spotted earlier. Three Montana guys put me, a lowly out-of-state tourist hunter, to shame the very next night. They welcomed me to their campfire and entertained me with priceless tales of growing up and hunting in Montana. They even initiated me into their One-Shot, One-Kill Club. Thank you, Jim, Steve, and Duane. Forgive me, Mr. Washington Guy.

10. Don't be afraid to do what you do best

A snowstorm headed my way four days into the hunt. It threatened to turn the backcountry roads into a slippery, impassable mire of snow and sticky Montana gumbo mud. I considered my options and made an early morning foray into the willow and cottonwood thickets of the Missouri River bottoms. This is whitetail country. I'm from Minnesota. I know how to hunt whitetails, face to face, in thick cover, in bad weather.

I still hunted upwind at first light and spotted an unaware adult whitetail, just yards away, feeding with its head down and hidden in the tall grass. It didn't matter to me if the deer was a record buck or "just" a doe. I had experienced a quality deer hunt, on my own terms, in remote beautiful country, chasing spooky mule deer bucks across ravines, fossil beds and former Lewis and Clark campsites. When the sights settled on the near shoulder, I did not hesitate to pull the trigger.

The Land of the Tape People

The Land of the Tape People

I topped a ridge on the rutted dirt road and braked the truck to a stop to admire and laugh at the scene laid out before me. I'm pretty sure versions of this have been painted many times over the last hundred years and maybe even showed up on the cover of an outdoor magazine or two. Below me, on the high bank side of the Missouri River, was a single tent, a well-used pickup, and a campfire. Sprawled in a chair by the lazy smoke of the fire was a tired hunter, feet propped up, eyes closed, napping in the midday October sun. Standing on a sand bar on the opposite side of the river was a mighty nice bull elk in all his antlered glory.

The bull seemed to realize that the blissfully unaware hunter and I were licensed only for bow hunting and posed no real threat. He eyed me arrogantly and took his time sauntering back into the willows of the river bottom. I shook my head and drove on, quietly as to not awake the sleeping guy. The encounter did offer hope. I hadn't started hunting and had already seen a trophy elk.

My first elk archery license was safely tucked away in my pack, one of the thousands issued by Montana Fish, Wildlife, and Parks for the Missouri Breaks areas. If you care about elk hunting in Montana, you have heard about the controversial changes in archery licenses for the Breaks. Once unlimited, they now require you winning a license lottery.

Hunting Around

Those in favor of the changes argue for a limited number of licenses, citing the disproportionate harvest of bull elk by archers and steadily increasing hunting pressure. Those on the opposite side make a case for continued open access to the elk herd on public and private land. They might mention the license revenues too. I wasn't here to argue. I was out to form my own opinion and hunt elk. The elk part wouldn't be easy. I was hunting alone, on pressured public land, near the end of a long season. And to top it off, two days of rain and snow were on the way. Most of the unimproved roads along the river were about to become impassable for days. I parked the truck in a sheltered campsite at the foot of a coulee and climbed the ridge to scout while the sun shined.

From this lofty vantage point, I had a panoramic view up several dry coulees and back down to the lush cottonwood and willow river bottom blazing in autumn colors. The muddy water of the Missouri River rushed down a channel on one side of an island and oozed slowly around the back side. I heard my first wild elk bugle on this same island several years ago while on a solo deer hunt. Thirty-some elk milled around in the barren November cottonwoods while I watched and imagined what I could do with an elk tag.

No elk were immediately visible today. But there weren't any competing hunters either. I started fantasizing as the sun began its afternoon descent. My trusty old aluminum canoe was strapped to the top of the truck. Maybe, just maybe, elk were still hanging out on the island and the canoe would float me to my own private hunting

The Land of the Tape People

preserve. My wishful thinking ended when the boat parade started.

The first boat showed at midafternoon, a simple outboard with two heavily camouflaged hunters. They beached at a wayward snag and disappeared into the woods at the midpoint of the island. Next came a high-speed, high-tech jet boat, loudly announcing its arrival with a throaty engine roar. Four hunters disembarked from its spacious confines and were quickly swallowed from sight by the island vegetation. More boats followed, each progressively confused by the lineup of boats already on the island beach. They hung back in the current, the occupants discussing strategy before beaching at less-preferred spots.

The parade appeared to end with less than an hour and a half of shooting light left. Then came one last solitary hunter in a small jon boat, cruising up and down the channel, indecisively considering options. When he finally dragged his boat ashore, a total of seven boats and at least fifteen hunters were on the same half-mile by half-mile island.

Even before the boat parade ended, the concert started. Elk bugles echoed out from all corners of the island. Most were easily attributed to archers perched in portable tree stands hanging above the willow jungle. A few were deep and savage, maybe real live elk, but more likely well-practiced hunters or guides hoping a bull might be dumb enough to ignore the amateurs.

An island elk herd finally showed with only minutes of legal shooting time left. I dialed the spotting scope in on a small group in a clearing. Three big cows and a couple of calves were head down, grazing, and ignoring all the wheezing, snorting, and bugling echoing up and down the river valley. Right at dark, a bull warily lifted his antlers out of the willows at the edge of the clearing. He too seemed unimpressed by the challenges being thrown down around him with the best scientifically designed elk calls blown by electronically educated humans. He remained in the brush, watching his harem until my cheap spotting scope could no longer cut the gathering gloom of nightfall.

I headed back down to the campsite and started my usual pasta and mystery-meat supper. The concert of fake elk bugles continued while I enjoyed the food, a good beer, and the stars from the comfort of a camp chair. I will admit to wondering about the purpose of bugling from tree stands over an hour after legal shooting time. The boats did not start heading back up and down river until I was ready for the sleeping bag. Only then did silence reign over the river bottom.

I crawled into my truck topper bedroom and snuggled down with one window open. I didn't sleep long. The real concert started soon after. Real live elk, bugling, snorting, mewing, stomping, and doing the wild thing. Some were so close I could hear the clatter of hooves on the hard pan of the road just fifty feet from the truck. I dozed on and off, listening to the show late into the night. It ended before dawn when the pitter-patter of rain began on the fiberglass roof.

The drizzling cold rain continued for most of the

first day, then turned to cold wet snow for most of the second day. Only on the third day did the sun return and begin the long process of drying out the gumbo clay roads. In the meantime, mornings were spent slogging uphill through the mud to use the spotting scope. If elk were hiding in the upland ravines, I attempted to slip and slog within bow range.

In the afternoons I took the much easier walk into the thick cover of the river floodplain, hunting the beasts up close and personal. I was alone, cut off from civilization and all those other hunters I saw the first day. The mud tormenting my aging legs created that private hunting preserve I craved, shared only by an occasional boat droning out on the Missouri.

The elk were in both places, hiding like heavily pressured whitetails in the thickest of cover. They erupted from cedar thickets while I rested only yards away, crashing off with no chance for a shot. They let me get close enough to catch their rank musky smell in the undergrowth of the bottomlands and then faded away without a sound or a glimpse of brown hide. I spent two mornings chasing the same herd of seven elk, trying to leapfrog ahead of them as they moseyed up a coulee. They played with me, letting me get within one hundred yards or so and then picking up the pace, and leaving me behind stuck in the mud.

They didn't respond to my weak attempts at calling either. In fact, not once did I hear an elk call in the light of day. Only well after dark did they feel free to finally let it all hang out, bugle, and carry on.

Hunting Around

The hunters from the pre-mud days had left their impressions on the land as well as the elk. I picked up a small bag of garbage from the grounds of my campsite and the roadside, evidence that some of them were careless and messy. Then deep in the river bottom I found what I dubbed "The Land of the Tape People."

It would have been easy to feel like a pioneer in this quiet, lonely spot where Lewis and Clark may have explored over two hundred years ago. However, I don't believe Lewis and Clark had plastic flagging tape at their disposal. The deeper into the bottoms I went, the more tape I found, marking trails radiating out from what must be a well-known hot spot.

Bright new tape, still fluorescing with hunter orange and hot pink. Old tape, faded dull with the age of years, still tied to branches and hanging on like the last leaves of autumn. The proliferation of tape had forced some hunters to become creative in marking their own personal trail. One used black and yellow striped tape hung in long ribbons. Another marked his territory with a rare pink and white candy cane striped tape.

But my favorite left me rooted in my tracks, pondering the possible tales and ramifications. Headed off through a tall grass swamp was a trail of white toilet paper, liberally draped over any available branch hanger. Creative use of materials at hand to mark a blood trail? Emergency trail marker when the batteries went dead in the GPS? I wandered on, wondering, hoping the poor guy had enough for its intended use when the time came.

The road dried out just enough by the fourth

evening of my exile. I four-wheeled out of the back country to rendezvous with acquaintances at a riverside campground. I was immediately sorry I had left my quiet little camp. Half of the dozen or so campers had generators droning, drowning out any possibility of a last quiet night listening to elk bugle and owls hoot. The fellow hunters I was looking for weren't among those present. The weather had forced a change in their plans.

A neighboring campsite promised conversation and companionship. It was a low tech affair featuring several old camper trailers, a campfire, and no blaring generator. I find I am always treated well in these situations despite my lowly status as a non-resident stranger. I was right again. Three generations of elk hunters welcomed me and offered food, drink, and a seat around the smoky campfire. There was talk among the younger generation, the usual bunch of male cousins, of the universal subjects of wheels, weapons, and women. There was also considerable discussion of the difficulty of the task at hand. No one had yet tracked down a bull elk.

Having had similar conversations around other campfires at this same location, I couldn't help noticing reoccurring themes. My hosts were concerned about the increasing number of hunters and the decreasing quality of the hunt and the elk. Outdoor writers were generally damned, especially those who had sung the praises of the Missouri Breaks to the masses. Montana Fish, Wildlife, and Parks took a few hits for a perceived lack of leadership on this issue.

But well-heeled non-resident hunters took the

brunt of the criticism. Specifically mentioned were a large group camped farther up the river. These out-of-staters were allegedly arrowing any elk that came in range and playing games with tags, a practice known as party hunting. While that practice is legal back in Minnesota, it's not legal in Montana.

Fact or rumor? Who knows? Unfortunately, perception can be as damaging as reality and as welcome as these guys made me, I couldn't help but worry about the future.

I headed out early the next morning, driving the back roads, looking for sharp-tail grouse and sage hens. Although I hadn't bagged an elk, it had been a challenging, quality hunt even though much of the quality may have been a weather-related fluke. How many more hunters and how many fewer elk would I have seen if the weather hadn't limited access? Would I be leaving Montana stressed and depressed rather than invigorated and renewed?

The answer to the obvious question was easy. Yes, I would be back the next time the license lottery gods smiled on me. Hopefully the heavens will align and strand me in the Missouri Breaks again. Or better yet, perhaps a near miracle solution will be found to the hunting pressure dilemma, one that allows reasonable hunting opportunities without undue limits on revenues, hunter access, and success.

And as long as I am hoping and wishing, I'd like nothing more than to return to the Land of the Tape People and find it tape free. Maybe more hunters will discover that a few minutes of practice with a GPS or a compass is a better use of time than shopping for exotic colors of tracking tape. After all, Lewis and Clark survived trekking through the same territory and I'm pretty sure they didn't even have toilet paper.

The Montana Mud Dance

The Montana Mud Dance

I was prepared for just about everything on my solo Missouri Breaks elk hunt. The terrain would be rough and the weather would be bad. Thus my trusty four-wheel-drive truck was loaded with enough supplies and equipment to make any "reality" TV survival expert envious. This paid off when rain, then snow, turned the twelve miles of dirt road behind me into a slippery impassable mess of Montana gumbo clay. Four-wheel-drive or not, my supplies and I were stranded for days. Stranded alone for days in some of the best elk country in the world. Stranded for days, all by myself, with thousands of acres and thousands of elk.

While I might have been prepared to ride out the Apocalypse, I wasn't prepared for the effect of the gooey mud on my mind and body. Not just any mud. Muddy, sticky, slippery Montana mud. I was in damn good shape for a male of the species over half-a-decade old, but walking level dry trails, and working out on various exercise torture machines had been done without the healthful benefits of Montana mud. Muddy, sticky, gooey Montana mud.

I dealt with it for four days of mud-bound solitude and was forced to become a connoisseur of the three basic types of Montana mud. The least common type of mud, and the absolute worst to hike in while carrying bow, camera, binoculars, and backpack, is the shiny, silver-gray ooze found on flat undrained tops of ridges and plateaus. This is a goo from hell that sucks at your feet as you slip and stagger across it. Avoiding it by scrambling horizontally across muddy hillsides is worth the effort and the danger of sliding back down the muddy hillside you just laboriously climbed.

On those muddy hillsides, you will find two other types of mud. The best is the charcoal black, grainy textured stuff. It may be wet and it may be slightly slippery, but it won't stick and clog. I learned to search out this dark mud whenever possible. Unfortunately, it only occurs in horizontal bands across the slopes of steep coulees. Sooner or later the band will peter out, forcing a move up or down out of your comfort zone. Here you meet the wet, heavy, sticky curse of the Missouri Breaks.

This mud is the common olive-gray paste that exists everywhere the two less common muds aren't. It sticks to everything it touches. Boots are easy targets of opportunity. Expensive, ultra-light size elevens soon resemble mud-covered snow shoes weighing double digits each. Avoiding this mud is impossible unless you are willing to sit in camp with your feet in the air and allow those precious deer and elk license tags to mildew in the backpack. The only reasonable option is to do what I did. You learn the Montana Mud Dance.

I personally choreographed this dance while staggering and slipping across the coulees above the Missouri River. That ballroom dancing class I took in college some thirty years ago finally paid off. I highly suggest the same for any hunter considering a foray into this territory. Who knows, you might even meet a cute, petite Canadian dance partner. But I digress.

Here's the basics. Grab your weapon and accouterments and head for the hills. Sooner, not later, those boots will turn to lead. Looking down will confirm that once dry and clean, the boots have doubled in size and weight, caked with olive-gray mud and assorted attached uprooted grasses. It's decision time. Either soldier on like a nimrod Frankenstein or do the Montana Mud Dance, a four-step maneuver that rivals the mambo or tango in complexity.

Stop at the nearest level and stable spot you can find. The first step is called "The Slide." Firmly plant your right, mud-encased foot. Pull your left mud-encased foot from the muck and slide it down the inside side of the right mud-encased boot. Firmly stomp down on the mud mass sticking out from the right boot. Now carefully lift the right boot while balancing precariously on the left foot, thus partially detaching the muddy mess. Now you're not done yet. True Montana mud will not give up this easy, especially if you're over fifty, dressed for bad weather, and not quite as limber as you were back in those college dance class days.

Replant your right foot, keeping the weight to the outside to avoid reattaching the loosened inside mud. Now comes the most delicate step—"The Reverse Slide." Carefully raise your left boot, swing it around the front of the right foot, and delicately step down on the mud sticking out from the outside. Lift the right boot while standing tippy toe on the left. Properly executed, this will leave a flap of mud and assorted attached vegetation hanging from the right boot.

Now it's time for "The Shake." Rotate the right foot around the back of your still muddy left foot. Bend that knee back so that the right boot and partially dislodged mud flap are extended behind. Now shake that foot! With a little luck and proper execution, the mud flap will shake off and provide tremendous, if only temporary relief.

In all honesty, The Shake might further loosen but not completely dislodge the mud flap. Now let's perform "The Kick." Cock that foot behind you, then vigorously kick forward. With any luck at all, the mud flap will sail off downslope like a muddy Frisbee.

Now you've got one boot free of mud. Congratulations! Do the same in reverse for the left boot, take ten steps, and repeat. Now you're doing the Montana Mud Dance!

Cautionary Note—Early in the process of learning the Dance, you might be tempted to move directly to the Kick instead of performing the Slide, Reverse Slide, and Shake. DON'T! Without loosening the massive mud mass via the Slide and the Shake steps, the mud will not dislodge with the Kick. The result can be anything from a loosely tied boot parting company and flying down the muddy hill, to a hyper-extended knee and the need for reconstructive surgery. Neither are acceptable outcomes. That need for surgery thing can be a real problem when hunting alone in an area of questionable cell phone coverage.

The Montana Mud Dance

Before you question my sanity for hunting in these conditions, let me assure you I had those same thoughts, in the rain and mud, on the first day of the hunt. These doubts increased on the second day, as I perfected the Montana Mud Dance on the ridges above camp in the snow and the mud. These thoughts were forgotten when an elk appeared in my spotting scope.

Over a mile away, on the muddy slope of a coulee, was one of the thousands of elk I had traveled here to meet. With it were four more, including a large-bodied beast that stayed hidden in the pines. Five elk, thousands of feet away, across the steep mud-covered slopes of the Missouri Breaks. Now was not the time to be thinking about sanity. I strapped on my backpack, picked up my bow, and got ready for a long, slow, muddy dance.

Just a Cow

About seventy-five years' worth of pure lean Montana cowboy climbed out of the noisy diesel pickup idling at the two-pump gas station. He tucked his hat-adorned head against the wind, cupped hands to light a smoke, and sauntered on over to my pickup.

"So," he said, a statement, not a question. "You're from Minnesota."

I'd spent enough time in Montana to know what came next. "Yup," I replied. "And I bet you are too."

That leathered face easily cracked a smile. "How'd you figure that out?"

"Easy—seems like half of Montana is from Minnesota and the other half has relatives there. I talk to a lot of folks who notice my license plates."

"I was from the southeast river country," he offered. "Been here a long time though. So what're you going to do with that canoe?"

The beat-up aluminum canoe strapped on top of my truck was as big a conversation starter as my Minnesota plates. "I've got a cow elk tag for one of the river areas. It might be easier to paddle a dead elk back to camp than to pack it."

The old cowboy contemplated the canoe for a moment. "That sounds like a lot of work, for just a cow."

"If I get one, it'll be my first and I don't care if it is just a cow." I pointed to the horse trailer hitched to his pickup. "Looks like you're in for some work too. Rounding up stock?"

His comeback was quick and enthusiastic. "No work today! I've got horses and my partner has an elk tag. We're going for a ride! We'll lend a hand if we run across you. You might need it!"

"It's a deal!" We shared a laugh, shook hands, and parted ways. I paid for topping off the gas tank and headed out across country, hoping I would be like that cowboy twenty years from now. Still spry and still hunting elk.

The familiar two-track dirt road wound its way up, down, and around twenty-five miles of Montana bluffs, ravines, and foothills. I took my time, stopping here and there to admire the green-gray coulees and the river gleaming in the midday sun far below. My favorite campsite in a sheltered coulee a half-mile from the river, was unoccupied and looked like it hadn't been used since rain and snow marooned me there two years ago. I parked the truck and got out. That was it. When you are hunting by yourself and living in your truck, setting up camp is an uncomplicated matter.

I didn't expect to stumble across an elk with only a few hours of daylight left. But a hike uphill with the spotting scope might provide info to jump start a morning hunt. I stuffed essentials in my day pack and dug the rifle out of two days' worth of truck-cab travel clutter. Like the canoe, the rifle might raise a few eyebrows. I was toting a sporterized 6.5X55 Husqvarna Mauser, a deadly accurate deer gun, stoked with high-test bonded bullet ammo. The ammo was also Swedish, imported at the cost of about three bucks a round. This light-recoil, low-noise rifle should be up to the task as long as I didn't flinch at the cost of the ammo every time I pulled the trigger.

Three months' worth of climbing stairs during lunch break paid off as I ascended the ridge behind the camp. I reached the crest of the ridge without passing out and slowly worked up the spine. There were plenty of fresh elk and deer tracks imprinted in the trail. The animals themselves stayed hidden. Archery season had been open for over a month, the firearm season for over a week, and these public land critters were no fools.

The boulder beneath the scrubby pine was still where I left it two years ago. I sat down with my back against it and alternated between binoculars and spotting scope, peering down into the leafless willows and cottonwoods along the river and up the coulee into the evergreen thickets. Nothing showed until the glow of the last hour of light settled across the valley. First one small bunch of elk, then another, appeared in clearings far below me. I mentally marked their locations and headed back down the ridge in the twilight.

Supper was a quick one-burner, one-pan, and one-fork pasta dish cooked up on the tailgate under a cloudless starry sky. Coyotes howling in the hills and the occasional bull elk bugling below along the river added plenty of ambiance to the simple meal. Then I buttoned up in the pickup topper for a restless night.

It might be just a cow tag I was carrying but I was excited and anxious anyway. After unsuccessfully bow hunting here and watching elk other years when there was no license, I finally had a chance with a rifle in my hands.

Sunrise found me shivering in a twenty-degree morning, down in the valley, hoping the elk would wander past before bedding down. That didn't happen. What did happen was one of the more memorable morning scenes I've seen in over forty-five years afield. As the sun fought to melt through the foggy valley to the east, a near full moon slowly, perfectly, set into the river to the west. And just when it couldn't get any prettier, a precise formation of goldeneye ducks ripped down river out of the moon and dove into that foggy sunrise. Somebody, paint me that picture. Please!

After an honorable amount of time freezing in the morning chill, I hiked back to camp and brewed a pot of coffee on the tailgate. The first cup was being poured when a white flatbed pickup with Montana plates bumped down the road. I waved the coffee pot and the truck stopped. A guy ten years my junior got out and wandered over to share a cup. The conversation went down some familiar roads. He had relatives in Minnesota and he wondered what the canoe was all about.

"I've got a cow tag too," he mentioned. "But I haven't seen an elk in three days. Where do they hang out around here?"

I told him where I'd seen them before. "They seem to be either way back up the coulees in the thick pines or down in the valley in the willows."

He gauged the half-mile hike down into the valley

and steep climb up the ridge behind camp. "Man, I don't know," he said, shaking his head. "I don't feel like working that hard for just a cow. Maybe I can find one closer to the road." He thanked me for the coffee and headed off on his road hunt.

He left me wondering why other hunters seemed to think I was being overly energetic and unorthodox in pursuit of a cow elk. In my mind, a cow elk was much better than no elk and using my canoe seemed even more logical. After all, humping elk parts back to a canoe and paddling a Montana river was not much different than paddling and portaging in Minnesota's Boundary Waters Canoe Area Wilderness. And people pay big money for that privilege.

By early afternoon I was back in the river bottoms, sneaking along the edge of the thick willows until I found a comfortable seat on a dead log overlooking a cottonwood grove. A windy day got quieter as daylight dimmed in the valley. Ravens, magpies, and eagles all made appearances. Then the magic of that last hour of light reoccurred. First a single raghorn bull appeared, ghosting along the border of the cottonwoods two hundred yards out. Then two drab gray shapes followed, heads down, silently grazing in the leaf litter.

I carefully checked them in the scope, making sure they were just cows—not bulls, spikes, calves, or even close-up whitetails tricking me in the fading light. When one paused in an opening, I calmly squeezed the light trigger on the Mauser.

One of the benefits, or curses, of a light-recoiling

rifle, is seeing results instantly through the scope instead of after a blasting recoil. A surprised elk looked down the lane between the cottonwoods, spotted me frantically working the bolt for a second round, and whirled away into the willows. It left no blood behind.

An extremely frustrated elk hunter fought his way back through the dark thickets of the valley, and took the long walk back to camp for a restless night spent second-guessing his equipment and his abilities.

I crawled out of the truck at dawn to find the valley blanketed in a thick creamy fog. While the fog slowly thinned with the rising sun, I made a hot breakfast, organized supplies, and finally, checked the zero of that rifle.

I paced off fifty yards up the coulee and anchored down an empty box from my stock of craft beers. The rifle was rested on the truck hood and two rounds of expensive imported ammo went downrange towards the label on the box. Two neat little 6.5 mm holes appeared, almost touching, just high of the label.

The willows were still thick and covered with cold damp frost when I trekked back to the site of last night's shot. The shooting lane seemed clear and the distance a little shorter in the full light. But there was nothing to indicate that the elk had not departed perfectly healthy. After an hour of walking in circles, vainly searching in the melting frost, I stopped to ponder my next move.

Something moved in the shadows back along the periphery of willows. The buckskin rump of an elk shined briefly in the sun. I dropped to one knee and tried to find the animal in the cluttered shadows two hundred yards away. A cow elk obligingly stepped into the cottonwoods and started a slow steady walk straight at me. At least ten more appeared behind, following the leader through the trees. In the middle of the herd walked a massive bull with sunlit antlers shining brightly way up high above the cows.

I hunkered down in the wet grass, brought the gun up, and promptly fogged the scope with a careless breath. I frantically rubbed it clean with a sleeve while the herd advanced on me. Cow elk fever again? Yes, I had it bad—shakes and all. I could have taken a shot at one-hundred-fifty yards. I had another chance between trees at about one hundred as the leader and the herd kept coming at a purposeful walk. I waited, wondering what would go wrong this time.

At fifty yards the lead cow stopped and turned broadside with the grass of the bottomland up to her belly and frost sparkling in the sun on the willows behind her. I put the crosshairs directly on the shoulder and pulled the trigger one more time. I imagine the shot echoed loudly down the river valley. I didn't hear it or feel the recoil. The elk went down hard into the grass while the rest of the herd scattered in front of me. I quickly moved in and fired once more at close range, just in case.

There was no fist-pumping victory dance, no whooping, or self-back slapping. I simply sat down on a cottonwood log and unashamedly admired this elk and the beauty of a November morning in Montana elk country. Yes, it was just a cow. A big old beautiful cow with frost still clinging to the long brown hair between her ears and her wet hide shining in the bright morning sun.

It took most of the day to separate the quarters, bone out the other good parts, and pack them to my canoe for a mile-long paddle up river. Then came the long walk back to camp to get the truck. I wasn't a pretty sight, walking the dirt road with elk blood liberally splashed on clothes, boots, hands, and probably my face. Two kids in a van stopped and told me so.

"You look like you murdered something with an axe!" said the twenty-year-old behind the wheel. "What'd you get?"

"A nice big cow back down in the willows this morning. Took me all day to get it back to the landing with my canoe." I waited for the inevitable reply.

"Down in that mess? That sounds like a lot of work for a cow!" He paused. "You need any help?"

I laughed and waved them off. "You should've been here four hours ago!"

The quarters hung nicely in a pine tree at camp once I got them there. I started boning the meat out and finished several hours later under the glow of the hissing propane lantern. I took my time, listening to the coyotes and the elk in the night and thinking about that old cowboy I met back at the gas station. I pictured him and his partner riding down out of the hills, leading a pack horse loaded with meat and a good set of horns.

He would probably give me some good natured crap if he happened by and heard my story. "Hey,

Minnesota, that still seems like a hell of a lot of work for just a cow!"

I thought of a response as I worked, just in case our paths did cross. It wasn't all that original, but I think he would have laughed and not argued.

"Yeah, it's hard work. But its good work when you can get it!"

The Victory Lap

Tag Soup. Most experienced big game hunters know what this means. For the less experienced, it refers to one of those hunting seasons when the freezer space that was optimistically reserved for neat white packages of large four-footed creatures, remains unfilled.

Hopefully there are memories of a frosty, sunny morning in elk country with bulls bugling just over the next ridge or of a big buck sulking off into thick cover at just the wrong moment. But other than that, all you have is an unfilled license tag symbolically floating in warm chicken broth. And, if it happens to be a non-resident tag, it's probably the most expensive soup you've ever made.

What could be worse? Well, how about a year when all your high expectations are dashed by losing out in the limited draw tag lotteries? Or worse yet, when the balance in the bank account doesn't justify the price even if the lottery odds are favorable. You could end up staring at the calendar with no hope until next year, no memories of a hunt, and not even a tag for soup.

I have faced that situation. When Montana's main lottery deadline rolled around, I couldn't justify sending off more than a house payment for a chance at a non-resident elk tag. Lest you feel too sorry for me, I should mention part of the reason was poor financial management. The deposit for a Canadian fishing trip was due at the same time and I had to prioritize. So I gambled on the cheaper cow elk and antelope lotteries and came up empty.

However, I was reluctant to let poor planning, lack of funds, and bad luck keep me from a western hunt. At sixty-plus years old, there wasn't time to waste sitting around waiting until next year. And I remembered how many times I had headed up a ridge with a rifle in hand and had ruffed grouse and blue grouse laugh at me from pine trees just feet away. Times when I was hunting lower and saw sharp-tails by the hundreds and coveys of Hungarian partridge erupting from coulees, spooking the deer or antelope I was stalking. There was also that time a couple years ago when the two brothers camped next to me were fishing and filling their coolers with big northern pike and walleyes from the Missouri River.

Thus late October found me headed down the road to Montana anyway. No bow, rifle, or big game tag was stashed in the truck. Instead I had a double-barrel shotgun, a bunch of fishing tackle, and a mostly deaf twelve-year-old Labrador retriever. I was also packing a fishing license, a small game license, and a waterfowl license.

The old dog, Kal, and I arrived at sundown on a Sunday night, the last day of archery season. The firearm season was still five days away, ensuring that we would have the area pretty much to ourselves. The hordes of archery hunters that usually frequent the primitive campground left me a prime site tucked in a corner with cottonwood trees on one side and the river quietly flowing past on another. The only other camper was a lone fisherman with a spacious camper trailer, holding down a spot at the other end until sons and grandsons showed up later in the week.

The dog and I never got to know this guy well. We were up before dark and back after dark, scouting my favorite elk, deer, and antelope territory. Without the pressure to fill an expensive non-resident tag, and with nobody to get in our way, we also explored new country, added some GPS coordinates for future use, and had a blast while doing it.

First of all, there were the sharp-tail grouse. While bumping down the back country trails on the first morning, my gray-faced, stinky-breathed, crooked-toothed old bird dog and I couldn't help but notice a flock of perhaps twenty glide across the trail and down into a grass-covered slope. We immediately parked and gave chase, the old Labrador quartering up the slope on her stiff legs. At thirty yards, about half the birds flushed broadside, giving me an easy first shot for the hunt. I am guessing the first barrel went several feet in front of the leader and was followed by an even farther off the mark second.

Sharp-tails have that effect on me. Their relatively slow flap-and-glide flight in the wide open spaces contradicts everything I have learned hunting rocket-flushing ruffed grouse and pheasants in thick cover. The rest of the flock flew away clucking in laughter as I struggled to dig more shells out of my pockets.

Those birds did tip their hand to the type of cover others were hanging out in. Sunlit east-facing slopes with thicker grass and greener sage brush were preferred. We didn't get our limit any one day. You can blame poor shooting and lack of sharp-tail hunting experience for that.

I did bag plenty of memories of grouse flushing in front of Kal and frustrating me with my inability to shoot straight while they clucked and glided off untouched towards the sunrise, the sunset, or the sun-bleached sagebrush flats. Luckily, Kal did taste feathers every day before crashing on the cot back at camp while I made supper by lantern light.

We started to figure things out on the third day. One coulee on the edge of the windswept prairie consistently held wild-flushing birds. We walked in on the western side, past an old log cabin, and crossed over and came at them from the backside. Kal worked upwind towards a mixed patch of sagebrush and grass, with her gray-tipped tail wagging. A sharp-tail came out low, fast and straight away, just like a clay pigeon at a trap range. It went down with a satisfying puff of feathers. That was an easy retrieve for the old dog.

I followed her uphill on the east side of the coulee, assuming there were more. A pair broke out high at long range and made me waste two shells. I dropped two more into the double barrel and snapped it shut just in time to send the first barrel off a long ways in front of a late-flushing single. I compensated and dropped it out of the prairie sky with the second barrel. We finished the walk back at the old cabin. A cell phone picture of my old gray-faced companion, resting in front of the cabin with the shotgun and birds, is my favorite of the trip.

There were also some ducks around. Stock ponds ranging in size from less than an acre to twenty or thirty acres were brimming with water from a wetter-than-normal summer. The ducks inhabiting these ponds were wary locals that typically rested where they had a good view of the dirt roads and flushed wild. So I noted the best spots and snuck into one under the cover of a dark predawn morning.

We ended up on the wrong side of the pond, as mallards quacked away on the far side in the early morning gloom. Somehow the old dog could hear them despite the issues that come with thirteen seasons of duck blind shotgun blasts. She quivered with excitement and whined as I held her back. Two big drakes couldn't resist swimming over to see what the fuss was about. My shooting once again limited our success. But one old mallard with four curls in his tail stayed behind to be enthusiastically retrieved by Kal.

In between the scouting, the sharp-tail shooting, and the duck pond jumping, there was the fishing. I caught two shovelnose sturgeon fishing after dark back at the campground. Small ones that I released but can now cross one weird-looking fish off my lifetime catch list. The walleyes I really wanted refused to cooperate. They were looking for live minnows, or at least that's what that fisherman at the other end of the campground was catching them on.

The goldeyes weren't so picky. I know Montanans and many other folk tend to think of these silvery, spike-toothed fighters as inedible trash fish. However, if these people were to check out the price of smoked goldeyes on fish market websites and notice the double-digit-per-pound price, they might change their minds and give them a try. Besides that, they were a simple guilty pleasure.

I grew up floating worms down a Minnesota creek, catching bullheads and carp. The same technique worked here on the Missouri River fifty years later. I tossed a simple slip bobber rig baited with a night crawler into an eddy of the river and caught a goldeye on almost every cast. Kal splashed around in the river at my feet, cooling off from the bird hunting and just as happy as if she were back on the dock at our lake cabin.

So, yes, it was the worst of times, the best of times. I got one year older without being able to pursue big game in a spot I dearly love. But I got to visit the wild country and keep in touch with it and the critters on a small budget.

And let's forget about money and the complaints about expensive tag soup. I walked the sage brush prairies, under the big Montana sky, with my old dog, for what was to be her victory lap, her last hunting season. You can't buy things like that.

The Rattler

The Rattler

The weather changed quickly during the afternoon, as the weather in Montana often does in late October. What started as an ideal sunny morning was ending with a low-hanging gray overcast, a stiff north wind, dropping temperatures, and more. Funneling south through the mountain ranges, just below those low clouds, was an aerial parade of every kind of waterfowl imaginable. Windblown formations of noisy honking geese. Long strings of sandhill cranes trilling primitive songs. Tundra swans lumbering past, hooting off-key. Precise formations of ducks quietly flying escort around them.

I could take a hint. It was time for me to head out or risk being stranded by the weather blowing in on that north wind. Unfortunately, the eight-hundred-mile drive back home would be done with an unused elk tag and empty meat coolers. As I pondered these sober facts of life, the elk appeared, a small herd of maybe ten cows and calves, almost a mile away across the valley. I watched as they faded in and out of the thick timber and then emerged one by one into an open meadow. They were right where the Rattler said they would be. But as far as I was concerned, they might as well have been on the moon.

I nicknamed or, perhaps more truthfully, stereotyped him as "The Rattler" before I even actually

Hunting Around

laid eyes on him. If you assume I am talking about a low down stinking snake with an ability to predict elk movements, you'd be assuming wrong. I gave the guy in the noisy Dodge pickup that moniker on the opening morning of Montana's big game season. As I climbed a ridge before sunrise, he cruised by below, lights glowing in the half-light. The diesel engine of his truck rattled away, echoing down the quiet valley while it spewed noxious fumes into the clean Montana air. I immediately labeled him as just one more road hunter and kept climbing, trying to put distance between me and him and the legions of others about to start parading down every drivable road.

It seemed like he had a tracking device planted in my backpack from that morning on. Every time I came down out of the hills, I'd see that blue Dodge rattle by. Or it would be parked down the road, watching, rattling away at idle, never quiet. And it wasn't just the noise. On the fourth afternoon, I drove down the two-track road to a trailhead and there he was, blocking the foot trail up the ridge. I was tempted to park down the road, step around him, and trek on up the ridge. He obviously wasn't moving too far. But that would have been in bad form and it looked like I was going to run into him again.

I drove past, fuming about road hunters in general, and particularly those in stinking, obnoxious diesels. Fueled by this funk, I let my writer's mind run wild with that "Rattler" analogy while I checked out new elk territory. Maybe I could come up with some humor story starring "The Rattler" and relate it so you didn't know if I was talking about some varmint snake or a person.

The morning after that encounter, I was up early, back at that trailhead, and headed up the ridge with gun and backpack at the first light of dawn. For a minute I thought the Rattler was gone, not out slinking around. Then I heard that infernal noise, faint at first, but getting louder by the minute. He was back, but at least I had beaten him this morning.

I turned, waved his way, and then kept on moving, working diagonally upwards along the ridge, slowly gaining altitude to take it easy on my almost sixty-year-old legs. His damn rattle was audible for about a quarter of a mile before it was blocked by the pines and rock. I almost forgot about him a half-mile later when the first mule deer doe and her fawn popped out of the cedars, bounced to the top of the ridge, and stood sky-lighted by the rising sun. I wished them well and hoped they didn't head back towards the Rattler. I wanted no part of his game, his style of hunting.

It was one of those mornings where the sunrise was warm, the scenery great, and I couldn't resist seeing what was over the next ridge. Before long I was miles off the road, miles away from the Rattler, and alone. A little hidden valley on the backside of intersecting coulees looked like the perfect place to drink some coffee and see what the early light would expose to binoculars.

It took a while. I was basking in the mid-morning sun when a chubby mule deer buck walked into a clearing below me and proceeded to make himself at home. He had a matched set of three-by-three antlers that were well below trophy size but not bad for this neck of the mountains. He also had no clue I was watching from above. He beat up some brush, kicked some dirt around, and took a leak, while occasionally looking over his shoulder at his back track, like he was waiting for something.

That something turned out to be a very nice mule deer buck that slowly cat-walked out from the shadows of the tall pines. Here was a deer that suffered from paranoia and probably had a few other mental issues—head up, alert, constantly scanning the terrain. He apparently knew his high and wide four-by-four rack was being coveted by many hunters not that far away.

The next hour was a study in the different personalities of individual deer. The big guy never relaxed, even when he finally laid down in the sunshine. His fat friend was the opposite, dozing unconcerned in the sheltered valley.

As interesting as this little interlude in the life of wildlife was, the time came when I had to get back to the business at hand. My backpack held a relatively cheap cow elk tag but my check book balance had not afforded me the luxury of spending six-hundred-some dollars on a Montana non-resident deer tag. There was no need to disturb these two and run them out of their peaceful paradise into the fangs of the Rattler. I eased back over the ridge and left them enjoying the sun.

I made my way down out of the hills by early afternoon, feeling more than a little smug and self-righteous. I hadn't scored an elk or even seen one. But a

The Rattler

peaceful morning in beautiful country watching mule
deer had to be better than riding around in a noisy diesel
truck, listening to whatever haphazard radio station waves
managed to bounce into the valley.

I was just lighting the stove back at camp for a
little mystery-meat late lunch when I heard that damn
rattling. There he was, crawling up to my campsite in a
cloud of blue exhaust. He stopped and rolled down his
window. I reluctantly shut the stove off and walked over. It
looked like I was going to be forced to deal with him one
way or another.

A guy about my age leaned out the window.
"How's it going?" he yelled over the rattle.

Since I have gray hair and an AARP card, I figured
I could get away with a little acting job. I cupped a hand
to my ear and yelled back—"WHAT?"

He grinned, reached over, and turned the ignition
key of the pickup truck to "Off." The rattling diesel
engine died a quick, if only temporary, death and once
again the air was still, quiet, and fresh.

"That better?" he asked.

"Yeah," I replied. "Much better!"

Now here's where this story takes a nasty turn. As
it turns out, I had the Rattler all wrong. Yes, he was
hanging out on the roads in that noisy blue Dodge, but it
was because he was helping friends and was bored. They
were hunting the hills via horseback while he tended
camp and took care of spare horses. It also turned out that
he had a sense of humor and was willing to share
information.

Hunting Around

"There's a nice herd of cows across the valley from where I was last night. Right down below where you walked in this morning. I've been watching them for three days. I even stopped a guy yesterday and pointed them out to him. He looked them over, said it would be too much work, and kept on going. What the hell do you suppose he's looking for? An elk that will walk up to his truck and climb in the back seat for him?"

We spent a half-hour trading stories and information before he fired the truck back up and cruised on down the road. He left me wishing we would have talked sooner or maybe even shared a fire at his campsite back down the valley. But that's not the only regret I ended up with.

I spent the evening back at the trailhead, thinking back on past hunts and watching the Rattler's elk, while the waterfowl streamed past overhead and the weather changed. In spite of my status as a lowly non-resident tourist-type hunter, I've never been treated badly by resident hunters, even the road hunters. In fact, almost ten years of experience had been quite the opposite.

I shared a fire and gourmet Tex-Mex food with three carpenters from Kalispell and their kids. Those guys had road hunting down to a science but somehow their company and their timeless stories of growing up in rural Montana overpowered the road hunter thing. I'd swilled cheap beer around another fire with a couple of twenty-something mechanics from Billings who rarely got out of their truck. But they kept me laughing at their campfire for three nights while providing all kinds of free advice on vehicles and some less politically correct subjects.

Another time I was welcomed to a humble camp by a family of three generations of ATV-riding elk hunters. Then just last year, I hit the jackpot. Two hunters and their wives treated me to a meal of grilled lamb chops with rosemary potatoes and asparagus, a meal I would have paid dearly for in a fine restaurant where it wouldn't have tasted nearly as good.

Mixed with the food, fellowship, and campfires of all these encounters, was the sharing of a wealth of hunting knowledge that I would never have time to accumulate at my advancing age. Yet in spite of these experiences, this time I had jumped to conclusions and put myself above stopping to talk to a fellow hunter, just because he happened to be driving a truck on a dirt road. And now this lack of manners was going to cost me. Those elk would have been easy targets yesterday, or the day before. But I hadn't seen fit to talk to the Rattler then.

Of course I'd have the memories of the hunt, including today's quiet morning watching the mulies way back in the high country. I won't forget them, and maybe next year I won't forget the Rattler and all the other hunters who have offered a lone stranger company and more. Hunting by myself a long way from home can get lonely. I'd better remember my manners next year and maybe even offer up the food and campfire myself for once. It's either that or learn to live with being lonely and probably elkless too.

Western Moments

There are two ways into my favorite Montana backcountry campsite. The easy way involves about fifteen miles of rough two-track dirt road. The hard way is about half the distance but there's a torturous half-mile climb up a one-lane switchback that always seems to be complicated by mud, snow, or ice. This October it was snow. My oldest son, Andy, was riding shotgun, hanging out over a couple of hundred feet of "elevation change" just outside the truck's door and clearly not comfortable with the situation.

"What happens if we meet someone coming down halfway?"

"I don't know," I replied, eyeing the next blind road twist. "It hasn't happened yet."

That moment was what I have come to call a "Western Moment." One of those things that occurs and reminds me that I'm not in my home state of Minnesota anymore. I've had many of these experiences over the years, even in the years when I haven't drawn or can't afford a coveted non-resident elk or buck deer tag. I head west to Montana, sometimes with my wife, her cozy travel trailer, and the dogs. Sometimes with one of my grown sons. Sometimes just myself and maybe a dog. Without an elk or buck deer tag, I'm there for the doe deer, or the antelope, or the ducks, or the sharp-tails, or maybe even a combination of those. I'm there scouting for next year's hunt. And I'm there for the western moments.

In this case, we made it up the switchback and through six inches of fluffy new snow. The payoff was a sweet campsite on a ridge with a panoramic view, sheltered in the pines in the middle of hunting territory. We scrambled to set up camp before dark. A cold front was rolling in on the heels of that fresh snow. Temperatures were expected to fall to historic lows overnight. Maybe even into the single digits below zero. It was time to get prepared first and hunt later. A wall tent and a wood stove would have been great options. But we don't have those. So our Minnesota ice fishing shelters would have to do. One for a cook shack and one with our cots and warm sleeping bags.

I won't belabor the challenges of that first night, other than to state that something always breaks when it's that cold. The bigger shelter lost a critical nut from a hub and couldn't be set up. We ended up packed into the smaller one, snug in our sleeping bags, still dressed in our best long underwear. It was one of those nights when the cold just creeps in and you just want it to be over. We survived five below zero, rolled out at dawn, brewed the coffee and went hunting. In this case there was no elk tag. I had a limited-draw either-sex antelope tag. Andy and I both had mule deer doe tags and upland bird licenses.

My antelope tag was our first priority. Normally we would drive a couple of miles to "Antelope Central," a high area with a three-hundred-sixty-degree view of thousands of acres of prime antelope country. You can usually pick out an antelope herd and stalk off down a coulee to intercept them. But this year the access road was blocked by snow drifts. Maybe we could four-wheel through them. Maybe not. We choose not to get crazy on the first day and headed off to scout other antelope spots. The snow proved to be a complicating factor in another way. Antelopes' brown and white coats blend perfectly with a snow-covered sage brush-dotted landscape. We didn't see a single antelope.

We did find that both the mule deer and sharp-tail grouse were on the move. Andy put a stalk on a deer in one coulee system while I snuck around in another. We both came up empty on the deer. The grouse weren't so lucky. They were congregating on the edges of bare patches of wind-swept ground and didn't want to move. We'd spot a flock, change rifles for shotguns, and put the stalk on them, wishing the whole time that the bird dogs hadn't been left back home. We bagged five of these birds the first day and four the next while missing more than a few.

We scouted hard between bird coveys and found areas that could be reached with four-wheel drive despite the ice and snow. With no antelope in sight, we went after the deer. We parked on a ridge with mountains looming in the background and a broad vista below dotted with pine tree-covered rock knobs. Andy wandered down the ridge with his 8x57 Mauser—"Grandpa's Gun." I headed up the ridge, towards the mountains, enjoying another western moment. I love Minnesota. But we don't have snow-covered mountains in the background.

I hung below one lip of the ridge, peeking over

while scanning openings in the thin pine trees. About a half-mile out, I found a trail beaten down in the three-day-old snow and multiple deer tracks headed down towards a creek at the edge of a sage brush flat. I stayed off to one side, easing out to the edge of the pines to glass into the valley. Five deer were spread out on the opposite side of the creek, heads down and feeding, about one thousand yards away. I closed the distance by dropping behind a ridge and then cautiously crawled through snow to the top. They were still unaware but well over three hundred yards away. I like them closer.

I eased down the ridge another hundred yards, creeping along with one last pine tree between me and the deer. I made it to the tree undetected and carefully scanned the deer. One was split from the others and closer. I got several looks as it raised its head from the sage brush and confirmed it was a mature mule deer doe with no apparent fawn. Now came the moment of truth.

While I've bagged deer, elk, and antelope with my sporterized Swedish Mauser over the last twenty-five years, this year had a twist. I spent more time at the shooting range since a friend had helped me reload my own rounds. When I cranked the bolt, a hand-load tipped with a 120-grain Barnes TTSX copper bullet fed into the chamber. I used a branch for a rest and settled the crosshairs behind the shoulder of the doe. I waited to calm myself, convinced myself this was just another shot at the shooting range, and touched off the shot.

The doe lurched forward, spun around in a circle, and flopped over. I picked up my day pack and made my way down and across the creek to her. There I took in the moment. A beautiful sleek Montana mule deer with snow-covered mountains hanging around for scenery in the background. I boned her out, stuffed the back straps in my day pack, and hung the quarters in a cottonwood tree. I'd have another western experience tomorrow when packing the rest out across the valley.

Andy met me back at the truck. He'd had his own experiences, stalking a doe in the rocky knobs below without an opportunity for a shot. But there was big game meat in the coolers along with the sharp-tails. Things were looking good.

We packed up our campsite the next morning and moved. The backcountry roads were melting into slushy mud and would be unpassable for days. I've learned over the years that mud is another part of hunting the West and there's no sense fighting it.

Our next campsite was in a rustic public campground on an all-weather road. The antelope were still laying low but we did find the mother lode of mule deer. Way down below where I bagged the deer, a herd of several hundred was hanging out around a large irrigated hayfield. Luckily the field and the surrounding area was either public land or private lands open to public hunting via enrollment in Montana's Block Management Program.

We scouted more the next day, then split up in the afternoon. I went looking for antelope while Andy put the stalk on a group of deer in a big sage brush flat near the hayfield. I'll let him tell that story:

Hunting Around

While not a true wilderness adventure, we were for the most part off the grid in Montana with the Missouri Breaks and Little Rocky Mountains providing a real western experience. My most memorable moment occurred midway in the hunt. I had blown a couple opportunities and was starting to feel pressure to actually connect. We scouted several spots and saw a group of four mule deer laying on a small rise, just the very tips of their ears sticking out of the sage brush. With little topography around them, they would be difficult to put a stalk on. But it was late afternoon and I was running out of shooting light and time.

Scaling a fence possibly gave away my position, but there were two small knolls covered in sage between me and the deer. As I moved ahead and peered over the first mound, I caught movement and saw they were on their feet and glaring in my direction. I crouched as low as my barking bad knee would allow and slowly wrapped around the next berm to the left. One of the deer stepped into range at seventy-five yards. Sure that I was busted, I quickly sat down. After several choice words, I peeked over again. Though alert, she hadn't detected my blunder and was actually moving closer.

The scrubby bush I planned to use as a rest was now perfect cover. I raised my grandfather's 8x57 Mauser and settled the crosshairs. The compass inlaid in the comb of the rifle pointed directly at the mountain I had climbed earlier.

With that mountain serving as the perfect backdrop to the moment, I held steady for the perfect shot. What seemingly took forever was over in a split-second. She dropped in her tracks, a quick, clean and humane kill thanks to the Nosler e-tip copper bullet. As I field-dressed the doe, I no longer felt the pressure of those failed stalks earlier in the hunt. They were now just a footnote to my western hunting story.

I got the truck as close as possible to Andy and walked out to help. We built a campfire that evening and roasted a deer heart and sharp-tail for a celebratory meal. The entire next day was spent looking for those elusive antelope and fighting the Montana gumbo mud whether it was driving or walking. We packed up the camp on our final morning and hit the road, determined to check every possible antelope spot on the way out. I didn't have much hope. But what happened shows there should always be hope.

We were several miles down the road, when Andy pointed to the right—"Look at that!"

A herd of maybe a hundred antelope was spread out across a sage flat, lazily feeding in the sun. We stopped over the next hill and surveyed the situation. All approach routes to the antelope were wide open and exposed. Except maybe for the south. If I could loop around behind a ridge for about a half-mile, sneak west for a half-mile, and then come back north up a coulee for another half-mile, I might have a chance. If they didn't wander off or get spooked by another hunter coming down the road first.

I frankly doubted my chances of pulling that off.

Hunting Around

But Andy pushed me. "Dad, you got to try. It's your only chance!" So I grabbed my day pack and headed out on a long hike with that old Mauser slung. The first half-mile was easy. The ridge totally protected me from view. I then headed west through a low area and ran into several yards of wide open prairie. The antelope, still close to a half-mile away, were feeding and resting. Would their sharp eyes spot me sneaking across this open ranch land? I hunched over low and slowly walked across, feeling exposed, doing my best imitation of a free-range cow moseying along. I dropped into the next finger coulee. The antelope hadn't moved. I hustled down this coulee to the main valley, starting to feel some excitement. Maybe I could pull this off! I looked both ways and scurried across the main valley and up another finger draw. The sun was starting to bake even though it was only about forty-five degrees. I cooled down for a moment, slid a copper reload into the chamber, and slowly worked my way uphill. I'd be within two hundred yards of the herd when I reached the top.

I stopped about twenty-five yards from the top to calm down. That's when a head popped up out of the sage brush right where I had planned an ambush. An antelope head, with horns, and a face staring directly at me.

I eased the gun up and tried to steady the cross hairs of a scope dialed up to 10-power in anticipation of a much longer shot. The antelope bounced to his feet, standing almost broadside. I didn't wait for him to make another move. I touched off the rifle and watched him spin away and disappear over the lip of the coulee.

I hurried to the top and surveyed the situation. Spread out in front of me at ranges of one hundred yards to two hundred yards were many antelope, all staring back. Big bucks, fawns, and does. Which one did I just shoot at? Where is he? Did I miss? I marched out onto the prairie, gun ready, keeping one eye on the herd while looking for a body. A white rump appeared at an opening of the sage brush fifty yards away. There lay the buck, down for good.

I knelt beside him, gave thanks, and took in another western moment. The beautiful buck. The rest of the herd warily trotting away through the sun-lit sage. The snow-capped mountains rising behind in the background. All once again reminding me that I wasn't in Minnesota anymore.

Epilogue

Memories

There is a saying, a few sage words of advice, that comes up often at writing classes and workshops. "When you see an exit, take it!" In other words, know when you have a good ending to your story, novel, or poem and end it there. Now.

I thought I had the ending to this book in the last story—"Western Moments." So I took it. But life keeps on rolling while I'm writing and assisting editors in putting a finished book together. In this case another trip to Montana happened. And it was a completely different trip than the one recounted in "Western Moments." We hunted the same spot in the middle of a drought and warm weather instead of after a snow storm and extreme cold. And we chose to bring along Tikka, Andy's nine-year-old Lab. Having Tikka with meant we spent as much time chasing birds as we did deer.

We had a great hunt in spite of the dry conditions and other challenges. After the hunt, Andy wrote a few paragraphs and posted a series of pictures on social media. In doing so, he wrote the epilogue for this book:

We didn't get the deer we were after; both of us had one rushed shot that didn't connect. The sharp-tail grouse were fun to chase with a few Hungarian partridge mixed in. Many chances at sharpies, too many, and just a couple at Huns, but we hadn't seen the latter out there for almost ten years, so that was encouraging. Also encouraging was seeing the number of sage grouse, although out of season. Their numbers seem to be on the rebound and maybe we'll be able to chase them for real someday. The mule deer does were surprisingly hard to find this year. Last year we arrived during a blizzard and they were herded up on the plains; one could pick their chance to stalk. This year the extended drought pushed them out of sight. We concentrated around the limited water resources and each day stumbled onto an opportunity, but instead of the many chances we hoped for, those two were it.

I guess we could have left Tikka at home and focused solely on the deer, but punching tags and bagging limits isn't always what hunting is about. It was her first time in Montana, hunting birds she had never seen or smelled before. Quite honestly, we wouldn't have seen half the birds we did without her.

Most importantly, I got to spend another week with my dad and dog, chasing birds and deer on the high plains, in the mountains and coulees of the Missouri Breaks in Montana. We had some good experiences, plenty of missed shots, but also saw things we might never see again.

And that's what it's all about. Enjoying the adventure and making memories. Until next time, Montana. We'll be back.

Made in the USA
Monee, IL
21 October 2023

44892866R00121